Revelation

To: Ms. Shirley

You are such a kind person and I love when we have our small talks at the random places we run into each other, such as Walmart. I hope you enjoy the book!

Thanks for your support!

Emily M. Triplett

Revelation

Reparations Trilogy

Emily Triplett

This is a work of fiction. Names, characters, places, and incidents are either products of the author's imagination or used fictitiously. Any resemblance to actual persons, living or dead, events, or locales is entirely coincidental.

Cover Photos by Kristian E. Colon-Bruno

Revelation. Copyright © 2014 by Emily Triplett. Published by Triplett Publications. All rights reserved.
ISBN: 1494851784
ISBN-13: 978-1494851781

For Mrs. Tara Dickerson,

Without her help, this work would have never seen the light of day.

ACKNOWLEDGMENTS

Family, friends, and the Collegiate High School's administration and staff are the reasons I continued to write even when I wanted to shut down the computer and give up. Without all of their support and kind words of encouragement, I would have never finished, and a half written first draft would have stayed on my computer for many years. My friends and family were encouraging from the get go, and for that I am forever grateful. The Collegiate High School gave me a challenge, my Senior Capstone Project. Without the push to complete a large scale project during my senior year, I may have never considered turning the idea I thought of one night into a full blown book. Thank you all.

CONTENTS

	Prologue	1
1	Training	6
2	Escape	21
3	The Chase	33
4	Reformation	39
5	Placement	48
6	Training	59
7	Discovery	71
8	Exposed	80
9	Interrogation	90
10	Clayton	98
11	Language	108
12	Information	121
13	Plan of Attack	135
14	Tortured	140
15	Jonathan	146
16	Aaron	150
17	Simon	157
18	Victoria	162

Revelation

Prologue

The sun shines brightly onto the vast field filled with colorful flowers. There are tons of them, some attached to bushes or trees and others growing from the ground. Small clouds dot the sky.

His little legs move as quickly as they can. He is chasing his brother. The ground shakes a little, but he doesn't notice. He can hear Jonathan, but he can't see Jonathan.

"Go inside! Now!"

Aaron listens to his brother, not sure what is wrong. He doesn't move.

"Aaron Stoppa! Now!"

He runs inside, not wanting to make his brother mad. After he is inside the little log house, Jonathan starts locking everything up from the outside. Aaron can hear clicks and swooshes. Jonathan even puts giant boards over the window, plunging Aaron in almost total darkness.

One candle is lit in the house. Aaron is scared. Mommy and Daddy aren't there. Why is Jonathan doing this? Mommy and Daddy said to never lock up the house without them. Why is Jonathan not inside with him?

Aaron sits inside the house, alone. He is bored and has nothing to do. He wishes Jonathan is inside with them.

Light shines into the house. A face appears before the window. It is a guy, and he looks nice. He has a kind smile on his face.

Aaron can hear the locks being undone outside the door. Finally he is free from this dark house and can play outside again. He loves being outside.

The door opens quickly, almost violently, and the strange man from the window is at the door. He is so tall he almost can't fit through the door. He is smiling softly at Aaron, and Aaron smiles back.

"Hi!" Aaron beams with happiness. He hasn't met anyone since Mommy and Daddy brought a little girl home a few weeks ago. He hasn't seen her since though.

"Hello, Aaron. Do you want to go on an adventure?"

"Yes! I love adventures!"

"Then we should go. Jonathan is coming too."

"Yay!"

Simon extends his hand and Aaron grabs it, clinging to it. He is so happy to be leaving his little house. He hasn't ever been allowed to leave.

"How old are you?"

"Four."

"That's cute. Oh, there's Jonathan. Wave to him."

Aaron beams and waves excitedly at his big brother. Jonathan doesn't look happy. Simon and Aaron walk over. They stand in front of a large car that can hold many people inside.

"We are going on an adventure Jonathan!"

"Yeah, we're going to have fun, aren't we?"

"Yes!"

Jonathan still doesn't look happy, but he seems a little happier than he did before. Aaron always puts a smile on Jonathan's face.

Everyone piles into the car. Jonathan looks sad, Aaron happy. Simon sneers.

"Aaron, look behind you. Say goodbye to your old house."

Aaron turns around quickly and looks, waving energetically.

"Bye house!"

He laughs. He is a child, unaware of the situation. Jonathan turns around and looks too, but not with the same enthusiasm.

Suddenly, their house goes up in flames and a loud boom can be heard. Aaron screams and tears flow from his eyes. He knows they aren't going on an adventure anymore. Jonathan puts a hand on Aaron's back, and tries to console his little brother.

"I'll make sure they never hurt you. I'll die before they

kill you, Aaron. I promise."

"You promise?"

"Cross my heart, hope to die."

Revelation

1 Training

Thunder booms, shaking the compound violently, as if there is an earthquake. Light fills the room before it disappears. Another strike of lightning and thunder occur before Aaron opens his eyes. It doesn't take but a minute before another lightning strike hits the exterior of the compound and thunder echoes in the stone room.

Aaron calmly rises from his bed, ignoring the protest of his body to lie down and not move. His body is bruised and bloodied from training that ended a few hours earlier. As he puts on his old dirty tattered shirt, a sharp pain explodes at his side. He grunts loudly. Simon's brainless puppets broke another rib, possibly two. Simon's puppets were once people with their own will. Now they are all at the will of Simon, the puppet master.

Over the years Aaron has become accustomed to

walking around with a bruised body that never has time to heal. He can barely remember a time when he hasn't felt pain. He can only remember
one time before coming to the compound. It haunts his dreams every
night, teasing him, laughing at his misery.

    He is young in this dream, but not a baby. How old is he now? Sixteen? Twenty? Aaron isn't able to figure it out. He and his brother Jonathan are playing in a field. Aaron isn't sure of the name of the game; all he knows is he is supposed to find his brother after he spins around a few times. He is looking everywhere, but he can't find him. He looks in all the bushes and around the house. Suddenly he hears a tree move and he looks up. His brother is laughing at him. Aaron doesn't know how to climb a tree. It is unfair. His brother can always find him no matter where Aaron hides. Aaron begins to climb the tree and then the dream ends.

    Aaron walks out of his room and down the hallway. No one is awake during a storm. They are too violent and dangerous. Everyone in the compound sleeps during these times, the only times when they are guaranteed not to be attacked. For Aaron, this means no training, which translates to no pain for a while. He walks around the compound and observes the storm. The power it holds over the people in this world is something Aaron craves. He wants to be in control. He wants to have power over Simon.

    Aaron starts to walk upstairs to the snipers' quarters where snores bounce off the wall, canceling the booms of thunder. Long ago Aaron learned this room has access to the roof. He tried to escape using this method once. It is an obvious escape path, so he was found within a matter of minutes. The punishment that followed taught him to not try to escape again, at least not through the snipers' quarters. Since that time, everyone knows Aaron won't run if he goes onto the roof, so they allow him to do as he pleases.

    He could run away right now. No one would know until it is too late. No one is as tough as Aaron. Not a single puppet in the compound can be exposed to the storm and survive. This includes Jonathan. But Aaron can't leave his brother behind. Aaron is going to bring Jonathan with him when he finds a way. He wouldn't ever leave Jonathan behind.

    Aaron pulls a chair over from the metal table and uses it to gain a few feet of height off the ground. The skylight is too high for Aaron to jump to, but if he uses a chair he can jump to it easily. He takes a deep breath and prepares himself for the pain. He squats, straightens, and propels himself straight off the chair ten feet up. He grabs for the loose board that will allow him to hang until he can grab the handle that will open the skylight. He holds in a scream. His arms feel like they are going to fall off and the pain he feels in his ribs is indescribable. He has felt worse pain.

    He takes a deep breath and uses all the strength he has to hold himself up with his left arm as he uses his right to open the skylight. The whole time he just wants to stop, to give up and go back to sleep, to go back to the land where there is no pain and he is dreaming. When he finally opens the skylight enough where he can fit his body through, he releases the handle and brings his right arm back to the loose board. Aaron is always surprised it holds his weight. With both hands on the board, he swings himself back and forth and then throws his legs to the right. Both his feet land on the skylight and he quickly throws the rest of himself to the right. He lands in a crouching position on the skylight.

    Aaron walks up the skylight and sits down on the roof. He
hugs his knees closely to his chest, ignoring the pain it causes. This is
his favorite position to sit in. He knows he can die. Lightning strikes destroy entire buildings.

    Regardless, he finds the view beautiful. Lightning dances
across the sky. Aaron's eyes can barely keep up with all of the movement on the horizon as it moves from one spot to another. Striking the same spot several times is when the lightning is what Aaron likes to watch the most. One giant bolt strikes and then several smaller ones erupt from the ground and smoke slowly rises.

    Rain falls from the sky, pelting Aaron's entire body. The cold water hitting his body feels nice. As it runs down his face, it turns a soft pink, cleaning his wounds, removing the congealed blood from his cuts and scrapes. The wind blows making him shiver. Rain soaks through his clothes. He should go inside and leave the storm, but it's too beautiful. He can't take his eyes away.

As the storm slowly dissipates and the sun begins to peak along the horizon, Aaron knows he has to return to the real world. The world he despises, the world full of pain, suffering, hunger, and blood.

He can sit here a little while longer and enjoy the howls of the Gelchorks as they roughly fight with each other. Or he can walk to the training room instead of being late like normal. He will decide after a cigarette.

Smoking always helps him think better. It has nothing to do with the chemicals in the cigarette, but rather with the calm, slow, meticulous motions of enjoying the first drag. He always carries at least one cigarette in his pocket.

Unfortunately, he didn't think that through when sitting in
the rain last night. Aaron sighs heavily. He rubs his eyes and looks
into the sun. It is too bright. It hurts. He doesn't care. Maybe if he is blind Simon won't like him. Maybe he would be killed and finally escape the pain. What would that mean for Jonathan? Would he be tortured or killed out of rage?

He groans and pulls at the mop of black hair on his head. He stands up quickly and jumps down from the roof and lands two stories below on the grass, outside the Gelchorks' cages. His body only protests slightly. He has made this jump more than once.

When he lands, the Gelchorks stop fighting and look his way. Aaron looks back at them. Unlike everyone else in the compound, he can relate to them. They used to be normal too. They used to be innocent mutts that chased cats for fun. Simon used to call his dog Fido, before Simon ruined him. Fido was once described as cute, fun, and loyal. Now Fido and all of the other mutated canines have seams down the middle of their faces, allowing them to devour a human in five minutes. They have a mutated spinal cord that sticks out from their body. Flesh is ripped away from their body, never healing, exposing the rotting muscle and broken bones. The Gelchorks can't understand him. They only want to destroy him. That's all Simon made them for: destruction and misery.

    Aaron can't determine the time. He doesn't know how long he has until training begins. He hasn't heard any movement, not from the snipers or Jonathan, which suggests that it's far too early for training to start. A feeling of relief washes over him. He has more time to brace for the pain.

    He needs something to keep him occupied until training begins. Simon would be glad to know Aaron began training early, but Aaron's body can't take any more damage. He is already nearing exhaustion and his ribs are screaming at him with every movement. He avoids exploring the compound simply because someone would think he is trying to escape again. He doesn't need extra whippings and beatings added to the training today. As Aaron thinks, the howls and growls from the Gelchorks quiet down. They are creatures of the night and are winding down due to the rising sun.

    Cigarettes cross his mind again along with the new thought of something to drink. Whiskey can numb the pain and cigarettes can keep him occupied and calm. Aaron doesn't want Jonathan to know he isn't coping. He loathes receiving lectures from his brother. Jonathan can't do anything to protect him. This is the only way Aaron can stay sane so he can protect Jonathan.

The sound of the compound door opening echoes down the hallway. If a puppet is awake, he will hear Aaron, but he will not do anything. The others in the compound actually enjoy the down time. They are exhausted and tired easily, but Simon never allows anyone to relax. Normally, Aaron would jump at the sound, but he knows he is safe today. He decides not to close the door. No one is going to come in and do anything.

He heads towards his room. He isn't going to smoke or drink much, just enough to calm his nerves. Afterwards, he will visit Jonathan. When he reaches his room, he goes in and quickly locks the door behind him. He pushes his stone bench in front of the door. None of the puppets in the compound needs to know his weakness. They would use it against him.

Once his door is blocked, he walks over towards his closet. He isn't allowed to have too many clothes; Simon says that clothes are luxuries, and luxuries are for the weak. Every article of clothing is black, ripped, torn, covered in holes, and stained with blood. Even with his small amount of clothes, Aaron is able to manipulate the way they hang so he can hide the cutout in the wall. The puppets in the compound would never suspect him of hiding anything, so they never search his room.

Revelation

Aaron moves his clothes around and pulls out his cigarettes
and whiskey. He knows where to find more when he runs out, but he tries to keep some stocked in his room. He looks at both items in his hands carefully. He only has enough time to enjoy a little of both before he runs to Jonathan's room. Simon doesn't like it when Aaron talks to Jonathan..

The smell of whiskey hits his nose, strong and potent, like always. He wastes no time before taking a long gulp straight from the bottle. As it slides down his throat, it stings the inside of his mouth. He loves this feeling. He walks over to his old, broken, stained mattress and sits down. He rests his back against the wall and takes another gulp. The taste, the smell, the feeling work perfectly to put Aaron's mind at peace

He sets the whiskey down on the floor and looks at the lone cigarette in his hand. He puts it between his cracked lips. He realizes he has forgotten to grab a match. He begins to stand when he hears three quick, hard knocks at his door. The knocks are the signal that his brother is outside his door. A string of curses runs through his mind, words Aaron learned from Simon that would make Jonathan frown. He has to hide everything quickly before Jonathan comes in. Jonathan won't wait more than a minute before he enters Aaron's room without permission.

He grabs the whiskey and clenches the cigarette. He shoves
them into the closet, moving his clothes to hide the cutout from Jonathan. Aaron quickly lifts the two hundred pound stone

bench over his head and moves it back to its place under the window. He doesn't huff or puff, take deep breaths, wheeze, or have an increased heartbeat. Not even a single dot of sweat forms on his body. Within roughly sixteen seconds after the knock he opens the door for his brother to come in. Jonathan wouldn't suspect a thing. Normally
Aaron answers within the first ten seconds after the last knock.

Jonathan enters his brother's room. Aaron says nothing as Jonathan walks over to his bed. He just locks the door and leans on it. The two stare at each other. Silence between them is normal.

"Are you okay?" Jonathan asks.

"Yes." Aaron's responses are always short and curt. He would like to say more, but he has no words to describe how he feels or what is wrong.

"Do you know how bad training is going to be today?" Jonathan lies down on Aaron's bed, enjoying the comfort. Simon and Aaron are the only ones in the compound who are allowed to sleep on real beds.

"No."

"The rest of us are going to a village today. It's rumored to have five large pieces of Zentarium that are intact. Simon says if we obtain the Zentarium, everyone will receive a few days off, even you. I doubt they are going to give it up without a fight. Some of them are going to wind up dying. It's not like it will be hard to return.. Zentarium is surprisingly light, no matter the size. We should be back by nightfall." Jonathan speaks casually about death and killing others. Death is normal

Revelation

for everyone at the compound. Killing for what is needed is acceptable.

"What?" Aaron isn't able to understand what Jonathan is saying. All he understands is that people are going to die. Jonathan sits up and looks at him. Aaron can see the sadness and disappointment in his eyes. Aaron is always ashamed of himself for being stupid, for not understanding. Jonathan can't explain to Aaron that he is disappointed in himself, not Aaron.

"Aaron." Jonathan motions for Aaron to come sit next to him.

Aaron slowly walks over and sits down. "We are going take some of the power. We will be back tonight. When we take the power away from the others, you won't have training for a while." Talking to Aaron is like talking to a small child. He hasn't learned much since he came to the compound when he was four.

"Okay." Aaron shoots his brother a small smile, and Jonathan returns it with a smile of his own. Jonathan stands up and leaves the room, leaving Aaron alone.

Aaron knows his brother will come back. Aaron dreams of escaping with his brother one day, living in a peaceful place, being happy, living without pain or fear. Aaron knows his brother does what he does to stay alive. Aaron knows they both do what they can to survive so one day they can be together.

He has time to finish his cigarette before training and his brother won't come back for a while. He doesn't have long, maybe twenty minutes until training begins. He decides not to lock his door. No one will come in. They will torture him soon enough. He goes to his closet and snatches his cigarette and a match. He puts the cigarette between his lips and lights it, inhaling the smoke and the nicotine. He keeps it in his lungs for a few moments before blowing the smoke back out. He takes his time smoking, alternating between long and short drags.

He puts out the cigarette on the stone bench. The ash won't be noticeable because the bench is old and dirty. Looking at details would require caring, and Aaron knows the puppets and the puppet master do not care enough about him to take the time to look or care.

He steps outside of his door and closes it. The puppets in the hallway look at him. They smile. They enjoy his pain. He hates them. He wishes they were dead.

He takes the familiar walk towards the training area. He truly hates them all. He passes the Gelchorks again. They send a low threatening growl in Aaron's direction. He wishes he was one of them. They have companions. They have others who understand them. He is alone. No one is like him.

"Hello, Aaron. How did you sleep?" Simon asks Aaron while looking directly at him with a cold stare. Aaron isn't aware he has reached the training room. Did he run instead of walk? How did he not notice? Why does he run? Why doesn't he walk to prolong the time before pain?

"Fine." Aaron lacks a response to the question. His sleep wasn't good or bad. It was a normal sleep with a normal dream. His response isn't important to Simon. Anything Aaron says is an excuse to begin training.

Revelation

Someone comes from Aaron's left with a bat. He ducks. The puppet swings violently and repetitively. Aaron manages to avoid all of the swings. His ribs scream, his body aches, his mind protests. He needs to stop. He is already injured. Training won't last long. A knife whizzes by his right ear. That was a close one. He runs to the left and
right, zigzagging around, avoiding the knives.

Simon's puppets come from him at all angles. Left, right, up, down, north, east, south west, everywhere, they won't stop coming. He is already taking a beating. He isn't sure where all the blows are coming from. The pain isn't quick enough to keep up with all the hits and weapons. The old and new pains mix together, creating a terrible pain over his entire body.

How long has it been? Two hours now? Longer? Simon's laughter fills the room. Aaron doesn't scream. He knows it won't help. It will only prolong the torture. Pain slowly takes over. He can't fight

back. He is tired. Blackness touches the edge of his vision.

The world goes black. Aaron doesn't move. He can't see or feel. No one moves him. No one notices him. Jonathan and the others arrive back from their assignment. Jonathan isn't told about Aaron not moving. Everyone knows he isn't dead. Their patience is being tested to see how long he will take to awaken. Will Aaron be normal? Or will he be slightly different? Simon loves to see how Aaron changes every single time.

Every training session is another experiment to Simon.

He wants to see what Aaron will do and how Aaron will react. Aaron's abilities are always put to the test. Simon is constantly pushing him to become faster, stronger, deadlier than before.

Jonathan and the others successfully brought back the Zentarium. There were only a few casualties for the rebels, as Simon calls them. Jonathan is the only one not covered in blood upon arrival. The others find extreme joy in killing. Jonathan always feels shame wash over him after returning. Simon keeps his word. He gives everyone three days of rest. No one is to do anything strenuous. They are to rest and relax.

The sun sets on the day, and Aaron hasn't moved an inch. The moon rises and Aaron lies still, slowly and painfully breathing. A new day begins, and Aaron moves a little. He still isn't conscious. No one comes to check on him. As the moon shines brightly for the second time since the training, Aaron finally awakens. He gasps for air. He doesn't move. He breathes in loudly. He blinks rapidly. Quick flashes of memories flood his mind. He hurts everywhere. Blood has congealed all over his body. He is filthy. He is tired. He is ready. It's time, time for him to stand up, to face Simon, to leave, to say enough is enough.

He sits up slowly. He breathes in, then out. In. Out. In. Out. Then he runs. He runs out of the training area. He runs past the Gelchorks. Rage is flowing through him. He hates Simon. He hates everyone. He needs to leave before he is dead. Next time he might not wake up.

He runs into the compound. He runs past everyone. They barely notice him. He is running too quickly for them to see. It takes the puppets two minutes to sprint from the training area to the compound. It only takes Aaron forty-eight seconds without sprinting as hard as he can. He runs into his room and slams the door. He is done with this life he is living. Aaron locks the door. He stomps over to the old bench and throws it in front of it. The puppets can hear the commotion he is making. He knows they will laugh. They love to see him in pain. They love to see his reactions.

He throws all of his clothes out of the closet. He grabs the whiskey. He opens it and starts chugging. His throat burns. It feels fantastic. He finishes the whole bottle. He is going crazy. What is wrong with him? Why is he losing it? He needs to escape. He can't take it. He screams and throws the empty whiskey bottle against a wall. He is done with this world.

With shaky hands he grabs a cigarette. He lights it. He inhales. He breathes in the smoke deeply. He loves it. He exhales slowly. He repeats this until he finishes the cigarette. He does it again and again, until he finishes his last four cigarettes. He needs to. He has to. When he finishes, he sits in silence on the floor, looking at the broken glass bottle by the cigarettes and thinking.

He knows what he is going to do. He is going to make a plan, a plan to escape this place, Simon, the puppets, everything. He starts to think of the flow of the air vent, the way it moves and what rooms it goes over. He thinks of the weaknesses of everyone in the compound. He can escape one day, at the perfect time. He can climb into the air vent, crawl through it, and run. He can drop down into Jonathan's room and help him up. They can escape together. They can leave this place. They can run. They can be happy.

He will tell his brother tomorrow. He will finally have a chance to talk to Jonathan. Simon will be drunk tomorrow. Both of them can speak without worrying about Simon's wrath. Then the two can create a solid plan.

For now, he needs another escape. His two favorite escapes are gone. He sees a sharp piece of glass by his foot. He picks it up and stares at it. After five minutes of looking at it from all angles, he slides the sharpest part across his wrist. The pain is dull. He does it again and again. Blood seeps from the self-inflicted wounds. Tears fall down his face and over the dirt, grime, and blood. He curls into a ball on the floor in the broken glass. He cries himself to sleep. Dreaming is the only real escape he has in this world.

2 Escape

Aaron wakes several times during the night. After the sixth time, he gives up on sleep. Blood has dried on him, his clothes, and the floor around him. He doesn't move. He just sits. He listens to the faint snores of those around him. He strains to listen for the Gelchorks. Not one of them is moving. They aren't growling or snarling. They are nocturnal creatures, living for the moon and the stars to rise again. Why aren't they moving? Aaron listens for a while and hears nothing. Something is wrong. Simon must be planning something. The Gelchorks aren't there.

Aaron runs to their cages and they are empty. What could Simon be planning? Gelchorks are capable of mass destruction. They can kill a small village in less than half an hour. Hunting and tracking are their specialties. No one can hide from a Gelchork. Does Simon plan to destroy another

village? Are there any left? Hasn't Aaron destroyed most of them for Simon's so-called training
purposes?

He can run around and try to find them, track them, and hunt them down. He decides not to waste his energy. This is a rare day, a day that can be used for so much more. He needs this day to recover. His body aches. The last training session could have killed him. He should take this day to allow his body to repair. A whole day of little movement can really help him. It can heal his wounds, and it may possibly save his life in the future. The next training session is going to be brutal. Aaron needs to be as healthy as he can.

He needs to return to his room. Reluctantly, he trudges back, dragging his feet. He needs something to do today. It has to be something that doesn't require a lot of energy or strength but will also keep him occupied until tomorrow. It takes him five minutes to walk back. A turtle or a snail could have made it faster, but Aaron isn't in the mood to care today.

No one is moving around the compound. It's completely silent. All signs of life are nonexistent. The first room he always passes is the common room. The common area always has someone in it, and if no one is in it, the room is locked up so Aaron can't go in. In this very moment, no one is around and the door is wide open. This is a rare chance. Food is visible. He is hungry. Food is a luxury and Simon doesn't believe Aaron needs luxuries. He sees fruits, vegetables, meats, drinks. He doesn't know what most of it is. All he knows is that it is something good for him. Is it a trap? Does Simon want to taunt

Aaron?

The aroma of meat hits his nose first. It's not fresh, but it's good enough. It could be weeks old, but it smells fantastic. He can't remember his last meal. He doesn't need a fork or knife. He grabs the meat and starts to eat it. He can't describe the taste. The meat itself looks brown, dry, old. It tastes heavenly. The meat has no juices,
nothing to make it moist.

A small memory teases his mind of the last time he tasted something so good. His mother is cooking. Aaron hears pops and cracks coming from the kitchen. She is making something that tastes good. It is meat. He thinks she said it is hamburger, but he isn't sure. She has a warm smile on her face as Aaron tries a piece for the first time. He can't remember anything else. It was so long ago, close to twenty years. The years of pain and torture ruined his memories of being a small child with his family before Simon took him and Jonathan.

Aaron can't find any whiskey. He opts for the purple liquid on the counter. It's dark and bitter yet a little sweet at the same time. There is no picture or word to tell him what it is. He has never tasted it. He doesn't like or dislike it. He drinks half the container. He still wants to fill his stomach. He wants to put more food in his mouth. He wants to enjoy more while he can. He sees small red circles with sticks on them. He goes to grab one as he wonders what they are.

Footsteps come down the hallway. Aaron freezes in his footsteps. He shouldn't be in here. Fear races through his veins. He darts out of the common room. Seconds later someone enters the room. He is lucky the puppet didn't notice him. He could have been beaten, whipped, released to the Gelchorks, or any combination of the three.

Why is he weak? Why can't he be stronger? Why is he afraid? Isn't he supposed to be strong? He lacks answers to his question. Why isn't he able to answer his own questions? He leans against the wall. Several puppets walk past him. The puppets and Aaron ignore one other. Aaron glares at the floor and launches himself off the wall as soon as they pass. He wants to destroy them. They would kill him. He starts to head towards his room.

The first punch is thrown. Aaron barely feels it. This must be a new puppet in training. He ceases all movement and begins to chuckle. The new ones never know enough about Aaron not to mess with him. They do not know why his training is so intense while theirs is so pathetic in comparison. One of the puppets, an older one, a wiser one, starts to yell at the one who threw the punch.

"You idiot, you don't piss Aaron off! We are no match for him!" Aaron turns around and looks at the puppet speaking. For once, one of them seems to know the consequences of what will happen. This one is older. Gray hair streaks his thinning hair. Small defined wrinkles cover the skin on his face. Aaron sees a faint scar over his mouth. This man must have been in Revelation longer than Aaron has. He must be strong if he has survived this long. Most puppets die within the first five years.

"Why not? I've seen his training! He always leaves battered and bruised! He doesn't stand a chance during training! He's weak! He can't do anything to us!" The new puppet is young and cocky. Aaron can tell. The last eight words feel like a punch to Aaron's gut. He isn't weak physically, only mentally. No one knows that. No one will take the time to understand Aaron. He is just a punching bag and occasionally a weapon of mass destruction. He isn't worth anything to anyone.

The new puppet starts to walk away. The older one looks at Aaron. Fear is written on his face. There are two others standing with the older puppet. They seem indifferent to the situation. They are dead on the inside. They don't care if Aaron kills them.

Aaron smiles to himself. Simon isn't here. No one will stop him. All the puppets are too afraid of him, except Jonathan and this puppet. Aaron takes a silent step forward, and then he sprints in front of the puppet. Aaron moves too quickly for the puppet to see. Hard sprinting allows him to be nearly invisible. He throws a punch. The puppet is thrown down to the end of the hall. The combination of Aaron's speed and strength allow him to cause an intense amount of pain, even though he can't fight very well. The puppet tries to stand and grunts. Aaron's senses are permanently heightened. Aaron hears him shuffle to his feet.

The puppet finally rises and curses before he charges at Aaron. The puppet is too cocky. Aaron decides to end this quickly. He looks directly at the puppet. Everything in Aaron's vision slows down. He focuses on the puppet's eyes.

Aaron remembers the time he was struck with electricity for the first time. He is seven. He hasn't gone to training yet. He decides he is going to skip. He thinks he is incredibly strong. Last week, Aaron thought he could start hitting Simon without receiving consequences. No one has come for him for days. He thinks he isn't receiving a punishment for his actions. Simon isn't going to come for him. He isn't in trouble. Someone knocks on the door. Jonathan tells Aaron to open it. Aaron is excited his brother has come to his room and runs to open it. As he opens the door, something attaches to him. Volts of power run through him. He has felt a similar pain before, but it is still too much for his body to handle. The world goes black.

When he comes to, he is in the basement. It turns out it wasn't
his brother that had called Aaron, but instead it was Simon impersonating his brother. He is strapped down to a table. The lights are off. He is in total darkness. Then it hits him. A flash of blue enters
from the corner of his vision before an incredible amount of pain strikes the left side of his ribs. He screams. It hurts worse than
anything else. Simon strikes him again and again and again. It goes on for what feels like hours. When Simon finally stops, Aaron closes his eyes and passes out. The pain is too much for him to handle.

The scar from the electrical burn on his left side starts to tingle. The memory rings clearly in his mind. He stays focused on the puppet's eyes. Everything is slowed down by Aaron's mind.

Revelation

"Scream," Aaron mumbles under his breath. The puppet is frozen three feet in front of him. His eyes are wide open. It looks as if a scream is caught in the middle of his throat, trying to escape. His body is slightly shaking. He is feeling the pain, the pain Aaron knows all too well. Aaron's purple eyes never leave the puppet's blue ones. He finally breaks the stare. The puppet can't see anything right now. His body is overloaded and blinded from the sudden pain. Aaron walks over to the puppet. He puts his hand on the puppet's shoulder.

"Relax," Aaron whispers in his ear. The puppet begins to collapse, but Aaron holds him up by his shoulder. The puppet takes quick short breaths. Tears flow from his eyes. He looks at Aaron and begins to shake. Fear takes over his entire being. Aaron feels no remorse. Aaron releases the puppet and watches him run.

Aaron goes to his room. Now with a full stomach and the satisfaction of proving his ability to the cocky puppet, he decides to rest. He should be looking for Jonathan and talking with him about what he is planning. He isn't sure he can do it without help. This may be the only way the two of them can escape together. He decides take a nap before he does anything else. He opens the door to his room and locks it behind him. He throws himself down on his bed and closes his eyes.

When he falls asleep, he has no dreams. He only sees blackness. There are no nightmares or memories that haunt his dreams for once. He falls into a light sleep. Any amount of sleep will allow his body to repair itself. He heals quicker than every other person. Twelve hours of sleep repair his body as if he has been on bed rest for an entire month.

When he wakes, it is late in the evening. The sun is not at its highest, but not quite ready to set. His room is silent, but the hallway is not. Laughter and conversations come in through the door loudly. This is rare and strange. Simon never allows the compound to be this loud. Normally his puppets can only discuss training, planning, or destruction. Aaron can't understand the voices he is hearing.

He sits up on his bed and tries to decide if he should go outside. They seem to be in a good mood. No one seems to be waiting to ambush him if he opens his door. He wonders where Jonathan is. He could be out there laughing. Or he could be sitting in his room alone, like Aaron.

Aaron stands up and walks over to his closet. He wants a drink. He moves everything around looking for it. Then it hits him. He doesn't have any more. He groans and hits his head on the wall. He should have grabbed some earlier instead of eating. He doesn't need the meat. He needs his drink. Why is he so stupid?

He cautiously walks to the door. He hears nothing immediately outside his door. It's all coming from the common room. This is strange. Rarely are there more than three people in the common room at the same time. Most of the puppets can't stand to be around each other. The only time they will tolerate it is during Aaron's training. He cracks his door open. No one is waiting for him. He opens it wider. No one is at the end of the hallway to his right. All the noise is coming from the common room.

Revelation

He refuses to walk to the common room. He knows better. He isn't allowed to be around any of the puppets in the common room. It is their room, their area to unwind. It isn't for Aaron to enjoy. The only time he is allowed is when all of the puppets in the compound are going out to seek out Zentarium or destroy villages. He isn't allowed to go because he's the best fighter. He is Simon's weapon. Simon likes to use Aaron at the beginning of a large battle so a majority of the puppets doesn't die. Simon could care less about the causalities, but he doesn't want to be left without some defense at Revelation. Simon uses Aaron when Simon pleases.

Aaron steps into the hallway and shuts his door behind him. He turns to the right and starts to walk towards Jonathan's room. He walks as quietly and quickly as possible. He is there in about fifteen seconds. Jonathan's door is wide open. Jonathan isn't there. Jonathan never leaves his door open. Aaron steps inside. Why would Jonathan leave his door unlocked?

There is a note on Jonathan's bed. Although Aaron can't speak well, he can read. Simple notes are easy for him to understand.

Aaron,

This is the time to run. Go. Be free.
I will catch up. I will find you.

<u>Destroy this note.</u>
~Jonathan

Aaron stars at the note in disbelief. He grabs the note and puts it between the waistband of his boxers and his skin. It crinkles slightly as he begins to move. He reaches up. He can't just walk right out the front door of the compound.

The ceiling is low enough for him to reach the air vent without having to stand on top of the bed. He loosens one screw and throws it towards the opposite corner of the room. It shouldn't be out in the open and visible. Simon is going to be angry enough when he notices Aaron is gone. No need to give Simon a hint as to how Aaron managed to escape.

He pulls himself into the vent. It is a tiny vent. He barely fits into the tiny crawlspace. He is malnourished and only slightly muscular, but this now works in his favor. He can maneuver slowly through the vent. It follows the exact path as the hallway.

It takes him fifteen minutes to wiggle through the vent. It ends in the common room. There are puppets below him. He can't come out yet. He waits. Ten, fifteen, forty, fifty minutes pass. No movement ceases. One hour, two, three, four, five and a half pass. He counts the seconds until they turn to minutes and then into hours.

He is eleven. Rain pelts his naked body. The temperature is dropping slowly. Rain turns to snow. He is chained to a pole, like a dog. He can barely move seven feet from the chain. He mocked Simon, and this is his punishment. Even the prisoners are treated better than he is. Simon has left him here for four days. His fingers and toes are blue. He is standing in his own urine and feces. He has no places left to stand, sit, or sleep on that are clean. He begins to count the time. He counts each passing second. He doesn't have any thoughts, just numbers flowing through his mind. How long will it take Simon to finish this punishment? It has already been twelve hours since he began counting.

Around the six hour mark his whole body begins to ache. At seven his head starts to pound with a horrible headache. At nine, all movement finally ceases beneath him. This is his chance. This is the

only opportunity to escape.

He kicks the vent's cover open and runs. He takes no time to look around the room. If someone is there, he refuses to notice. He runs straight to the door on his left. The door to freedom is right in front of him. He runs out the front door of the compound. He doesn't look behind him. He doesn't listen for shouts or growls. He hopes no one tries to catch up to him.

He begins to sprint as hard as he can. He is nearly invisible to the naked eye. Snipers may be able to see him, but he doesn't think about that. Any bad thoughts can slow him down. He must not slow down.

He runs past the Gelchorks. The only creatures he can relate to blur past him. He pays them no mind as they howl. He never looks back. Neither the howls of the Gelchorks or the thought of his brother even give him the slightest need to turn back.

He passes the training room. He wishes he could cause the building as much pain as he can humans. It would be the

first place he would destroy out of pure anger. He shakes his head violently. He must not allow himself to think of anything. He cannot stop or slow
down. He will never have this chance again.

    The last barrier comes into his line of vision on the horizon. He slows as he approaches the fifteen foot guard wall of the compound. This is his last obstacle before he reaches freedom. He wants to take one final look back, but he knows he can't. He wants to run back and grab Jonathan. He wants them both to escape, but he knows they can't. He scales the fifteen foot wall that surrounds the compound and goes off into the wilderness. Aaron is finally free from Simon and his puppets at Revelation.

3 The Chase

He should be glad. He is away from all the pain now. He is free from the torture. He is free. Free from Simon and his puppets. Yet, his heart feels heavy. He is missing something.

Should he have listened to his brother? Is it really the best decision? Would it have been worth it to wait? Could he have found a way to bring his brother with him? Why does he just act? Why doesn't he stop and think?

As dawn breaks over the horizon, light creates long shadows from the trees. The few species of flowers that managed to survive are visible. The soft morning light reveals the fresh blooms. Aaron doesn't care much for flowers. They die too quickly. They mean nothing. They can't help him. They can't find Jonathan and bring him here. They can't hide him from Simon.

A Gelchork howls in the distance. Their howls are loud

and pierce the ear. Anyone would know a Gelchork is within a few feet. The howl is faint, so the Gelchork is twenty miles away. Simon never brings the Gelchorks out one by one. The whole pack must be hunting him down.

Simon knows. Color escapes Aaron's face. He runs in a straight path, quickly and quietly, and leaves no trace. The only thing he leaves is his scent. He isn't sprinting yet. He can't afford to waste his energy. He still has miles between himself and the nearest Gelchork and handler. He runs quicker than the Gelchorks. He is safe, for now.

He runs. He only focuses on his breathing and taking the next step forward. He doesn't even consider what he will do if the Gelchorks catch up to him. Nothing concerns him.

If the Gelchorks were to catch up to him, he wouldn't hear them. He wouldn't see them. He can't fight them. He can only out run them.

Aaron needs to put as much distance as possible between himself and the Gelchorks. He takes all the difficult paths. He avoids any flat lying areas. He runs through ditches, up large piles of rubble, over fallen trees. Gelchorks only have speed when running straight and on a level surface. They can run over obstacles easily, but Aaron knows they have one fault. Gelchorks can't easily change their direction. If Gelchorks see the road suddenly turn into a ditch, they will have to slow down in order to be able to jump into the ditch and then run upwards to escape. If a pile of huge boulders blocks the way, the Gelchork won't be able to suddenly know whether to run around it or climb up it. They will stop and wait for the handler to determine what to do. This slows the hunt down, making it easier for Aaron to escape.

Aaron keeps running. Aaron knows nothing about the forest he is in now. When Simon would send him to a village to train, he would be escorted on a Gelchork's back. He normally slept, never paying attention to the scenery or the route they took.

He passes hundreds of trees and bushes, runs for miles and hours, and eventually stumbles onto an actual road. Not a dirt path, but asphalt. There are still trees everywhere, but a road means something. It means he isn't in the forest.

He stands in his spot. He doesn't move. He listens for the Gelchorks. They are nowhere near him. He's safe.

What will happen to Jonathan? Will they know he helped Aaron escape? Will they torture him for information? Will Simon take out his anger on Jonathan? Will Jonathan suffer for helping his little brother escape? Will Aaron find out one day that Jonathan has become a new training dummy for the Gelchorks? Or will Jonathan manage to escape by himself?

Aaron groans, pulls his hair, and falls onto his back. The sun is at its highest. It has been half a day since he left; half a day of freedom. He has been running at a constant speed since day break. His body will catch up later. He refuses to sleep.

Where can he go? He doesn't know much about the world. He doesn't know where he is. He needs to find a safe place to stay. It won't be long before Simon sends messages to the other compounds alerting them that Simon's weapon has escaped. Aaron knows other compounds exist outside of

Simon's main Revelation compound. He remembers Simon complaining one time about a group called Reformation.

Reformation is trying to destroy Simon and Revelation. They
are trying to destroy Aaron, too. Aaron has always known that if someone wanted to hurt Simon, they would kill him. He is important to Revelation. At Reformation they may kill him or they may spare him at first, then torture and kill him. Anything is better than Simon and Revelation.

Aaron looks up at the clouds, white, puffy, harmless. The sun is shining, burning his bloodied skin. He never cleans up after the last training.

He decides to go to Reformation. He stands up and begins to walk. He isn't sure where he is going, but he knows he will find it eventually. The road leads to the left and right. He goes right.

There is nothing on the road. There are no mutant animals created from exposure or radiation making any noises. The road is completely deserted. He keeps walking.

The sun begins to set, yet to Aaron, it doesn't feel like he has been walking that long. Does he dare stop for the night? His head has been pounding for a while now. His hands are shaking. He needs to stop, but night is the Gelchorks' prime time to hunt, to move, to lurk, to kill. He has no idea how far away the closest one is. They can be anywhere. He would rather die of exhaustion than slip into a restless sleep and not be able to run or defend himself.

He keeps walking. He walks through the night. He

doesn't stop. He can't wear himself out. He can't be completely exhausted and surrounded by Gelchorks.

The sun rises and sets twice more. Aaron has been walking for three days. He is ready to fall on the ground and allow the Gelchorks to rip him apart. If Aaron chooses to die now, Jonathan will have wasted his chance to escape on his brother who decided to give up. Aaron trudges forward. As the sun begins to rise again, stilettos of small buildings are visible along the horizon. This means a place to rest, a place to gather his bearings, a place to find out where he is.

He restrains himself from running. It doesn't take him long to

make his way to the buildings. Everything is deserted. He notices there is a gas station. They normally have food, so he walks over to it and enters.

There are a few canned items left. He opens them and drinks them. It's probably expired but he doesn't care. He heads to the cooler and finds a giant can of tea. It's hot. He drinks it. It feels good on his throat. He collapses against the cooler door.

He can finally relax a little and build his energy back up and sleep in a sound place. He examines his drink. The top part of the can is reflective. He notices his eyes really stand out. His eyes are a dead giveaway as to who he is. He crawls on the ground, too tired to stand. He finds the aisle with hair products. There is a box of blonde dye and a few boxes of black dye. His hair is already black. He needs to change his appearance. He crawls down a little farther and finds some contacts that are dark brown. They will work.

He also sees a newspaper next to his hand. The front page is filled with stories about the controversy of colored contacts sold at gas stations and grocery stores. They supposedly aren't good for the eyes. He doesn't bother to read it. He proceeds to dye his hair. The bleach burns his scalp, but the finished product is worth it. It's not like he hasn't felt worse pain. His hair is now a dark blonde, his eyes a dark brown. He no longer looks like Aaron the Warrior Weapon.

4 Reformation

Aaron feels like he hasn't walked more than five feet. He is frozen in time. No change in scenery or weather can do that to a person. He does the same thing every single day. Walk, look at the trees, rest at sundown for a few hours, wake, and walk. Nothing changes. He hasn't heard any howls from Gelchorks or any orders from handlers. He must be safe. They could have given up. Most who venture into the woods die from exposure within a month. Simon must think Aaron is dead. Maybe Aaron won't be hunted any longer. Maybe he can live in peace.

Aaron has stopped thinking about his brother. Aaron thinks of Jonathan's wellbeing, hoping Jonathan is alright. He knows he can't dwell. He only listens for attacks. He has occasionally sprinted as far and as fast as he can until he collapses.

Aaron hears rustling about fifty feet to his left. An animal is around. His stomach growls for the food. He sprints towards the rustling. He wants the meat. He hasn't eaten in a while now.

He runs into a clearing. No animal is visible. He shouldn't have wasted his energy. He didn't even know what it was. He closes his eyes and starts to walk straight forward. He covers his eyes with his hand, continuing forward while shaking his head. He is stupid.

He walks into something solid and cold. He doesn't move back immediately, but instead slowly takes a few steps back. He uncovers his eyes, and sees he has run into a building. He backs up a few steps farther, and looks at the building. It is a short shack. On the wall there is a dove holding an olive branch is painted.

Revelation bases have burning branches painted on the walls. Aaron has never been told what the symbol means. During his entire life, Jonathan has told Aaron that Simon's enemies have a symbol that is different from Revelation's. Instead of a burning branch, a bird holds a branch. The only enemy Aaron knows about is Reformation.

This is it. This is the place he has been looking for. He has found his last hope for safety. He looks around for any sign of the compound. He sees it. He sprints towards the compound. He is there within two minutes of seeing it on the horizon. Walking would have taken at least half an hour, maybe more, considering it is on a hill. Unlike Revelation's compounds, there isn't a wall surrounding the compound. Instead, the building is a long one story building.

He walks up to the door. His heart is racing. Sweat trickles down from his brow. His hands shake. Simon would think he is pitiful, shaking from knocking on a door. Why is he weak? Why isn't he fearless?

The door opens. A large middle aged man stands in the doorway. Anger and stress cross his features. Aaron stands, hiding any fear he may contain. This man could easily sense Aaron is Simon's weapon. He could kill Aaron on the spot. Aaron could be breathing his last breathe right now. A chill runs up his spine as the man speaks.

"Why are you here?"

"I want to destroy Revelation," Aaron answers.

The man looks at Aaron. Aaron looks at the man. Neither exchanges any words. The man opens the door to allow Aaron in. Aaron takes the invitation and steps inside. Before he looks around, two men in black cloaks come and stand before Aaron. They nod their heads towards the hall behind them. It's a gesture meant to tell Aaron to follow. He doesn't understand. They start to walk off while Aaron stands there confused.

The large man who answered the door pushes Aaron in their direction. He stumbles, but catches himself before he falls. Aaron doesn't dare look back at the man, but he wants to glare at him, send him into a world of pain, to show him he shouldn't mess with him. He can't ruin the opportunity he is receiving now. He can't give away who he is.

He decides to go against his urge and follow the men. Maybe they are leading him to his death now.

Aaron wouldn't be able to find his way through this building if he ever needed to. The immense number of hallways and oddly shaped rooms make it too difficult to follow. If this is his end, it should be quick. If it isn't his end, he hopes anything he hears won't have him running to the exit.

After following the men for a short period of time, they lead Aaron to a door. The door is unmarked and looks the same as the others. There doesn't seem to be anything special about this door. If they are walking him to his death, he expects a heavy metal door, like the one leading to the basement in Simon's compound.

Aaron hesitates. Should he wait or knock? Sit or stand? Breathe or not? He stands there. In the past, Simon has sent a few blows Aaron's way for trying to do something to gain his attention. Aaron doesn't want to be beaten today. He would rather look stupid than do something he shouldn't.

Aaron shakes his head and looks at his feet. He stuffs his hands in his pockets. He doesn't look stupid; he is stupid. Stupid enough to think he can escape Simon and be happy. He's too stupid to knock on the door. He can't ever do anything he should do. He can either do what he is supposed to and be beaten, or not do anything and be reminded of his stupidity by everyone that walks by. Aaron takes his hand out of his pocket and runs it along his left wrist. He can feel the scars from months ago. He starts to scratch them until a dull pain and red marks appear. He has fallen as low as he can go. Why is he still alive?

"You look new," a female says nonchalantly.

Revelation

Aaron looks to his right and is surprised by what he sees. At Revelation's compound, females only exist for the men's pleasure. When Aaron is sent to destroy villages, he never looks at females in any way except as moving, screaming targets. Never before has Aaron taken a look at a female and felt his heart stop. She is beautiful. Her eyes are deep and dark. Her hair is a light mixture between blonde and brunette and has been thrown into a ponytail.

"Can you quit staring?" she asks him. "What, haven't you ever seen a girl before?"

Aaron feels heat rush to his face. He knows he is slightly red. He would rather be anywhere else right now.

When Aaron says nothing, the girl sends him a weird look. He looks down at his feet. He wishes she would just go away.

"You're kind of weird. What are you doing here?"

"I don't know." Aaron surprises himself. Normally he doesn't say much.

"Did two guys bring you here?"

"Yes." The girl huffs and shakes her head. She walks right to the door and knocks, and then she throws it open. "Come on in. Clayton you have a visitor!" The girl walks into the room with no fear. Aaron takes a few steps and notices the room is a library with walls of books. One wall is a giant window, illuminating the entire room with sunshine.

The girl is standing next to a taller man. He looks around the same age as the girl. Both are young, Aaron knows that. The man has some scruff on his chin. It looks as if he intentionally cuts it to have it there. Aaron runs his hand over his own face. He feels like he needs to shave. Aaron can go long periods of time without shaving, but he hates it when he starts to grow a thick beard. He doesn't like it and wants it gone. That's what he has now. Surely he can find a sharp knife in the compound somewhere.

"Hello. My name is Clayton. This lady to my left is Victoria; I'm sure she forgot to introduce herself again. State your name please." Victoria whispers oops under her breath and begins twiddling her thumbs. Clayton has a deep voice. He sounds like an older man. There is no doubt in Aaron's mind that Clayton has seen a lot, especially if he has been at Reformation's compound.

"Aaron."

"Welcome, Aaron. Why are you here? Why did you come to Reformation, today of all days? Victoria, have someone bring tea for the three of us."

"Jeez, you are so lazy!" Victoria runs out into the hallway quickly, not nearly as fast as Aaron, but with impressive speed for someone of her short body size.

"Hey! We need some tea in the library! Enough for three! You have five minutes until I come and start beating everyone!" Victoria walks back into the study and calmly returns to Clayton's side. Aaron wants to laugh, but he holds it in. Clayton could be just like Simon for all Aaron knows. Aaron doesn't want to do anything until he understands Clayton a little more.

"I want to destroy Revelation."

"Why now?"

"I always have."

"Why today? Why not yesterday? Why not six months ago when their Warrior Weapon destroyed yet another village and killed six hundred children? Why not then?"

Pain crosses Aaron's features. Clayton knows what Aaron has done. Aaron must hide it. Aaron can't allow Clayton to know he is the Warrior Weapon. Aaron must stay calm.

"I couldn't before. I can now."

"Aaron, is it? Why couldn't you before? Care to explain why you didn't want to help then?" Victoria snaps at Aaron. She must hate him already.

He must stay calm. He must. Her words can't hurt him. Nothing can. He must not allow her words to hurt him.

"I couldn't. I was stuck. Now I'm not. I can help now."

"What do you know about Revelation?" Clayton heads towards a table with four small chairs. Victoria follows Clayton dutifully, almost like a small puppy, and Aaron take it as a sign that he should also follow. As they begin to sit, a young man in holey jeans and a white tank top comes in and sets tea on the table. As quickly as he enters he leaves, barely noticed by anyone in the room.

"Not much. They are bad. They kill. They take what they want." Aaron tries his best to state his point. He barely understands the question. His answers are horrible and short. They must think he is stupid. Why wouldn't they?

"Do you think you can help us? Do you think you can kill them? Destroy them? Hurt them without feeling bad about it?" Clayton asks these questions in a cold, deadly voice.

"Yes." Aaron says. There is no hesitation. Aaron knows he can. He wants nothing more than to see Revelation destroyed.

"I like you. Short simple answers are what I like." Victoria tells Aaron with a small smile on her face. This is the first time someone has said something like that to Aaron. It feels good. "Does he meet your standards Clayton?"

"We need to see his physical levels. He looks like he can withstand a march and a few battles. If not we will need to see his mental levels to place him accordingly."

"Are you good at anything in particular?" Victoria poses the question, extremely interested in Aaron now. She leans forward, ignores her tea, and folds her hands together under her chin.

"Yes, running." Aaron adds nothing to his answer.

"Just running?" Victoria tries to get a more elaborate answer from Aaron.

"Yes."

"That's all?" Confusion or annoyance is present in Victoria's voice. Aaron isn't sure which.

"Yes."

"Are you sure?"

"Yes."

"Do you say anything else?" Victoria is annoyed by now. Aaron can tell.

"Yes." Aaron isn't trying to be annoying. He does say more than yes if asked to.

The two are looking at each other, but neither says another word. Aaron starts to count the time. Thirty seconds, a minute, three minutes, seven minutes, fifteen minutes, thirty-two minutes pass. Aaron wants to say something, to break the silence. He knows he can't. Unless he is spoken to he cannot speak.

"Aaron," Victoria and Clayton speak at the exact same moment.

Aaron looks between the two, very confused. How do they manage to pull that off without making any signs at each other, without even looking at each other?

"Smart kid." Clayton says, "He knows when to keep his mouth shut, unlike a certain female."

"Clayton! You are so mean!"

"We will just ignore her. Well, I can ignore her. I'm going to have her train you. Maybe you can do more than run. Victoria," Clayton turns his attention to her, turning his back on Aaron. "Make sure you run all the normal tests. Find his faults, find his strengths. I expect a full report in two days."

5 Placement

Victoria stands and analyzes Aaron. Neither says a word. He allows her look all she pleases. He isn't sure what he should say in this situation. Should he tell her to stop staring? Or should he ask her what she is looking for? He says nothing.

"Well," Victoria finally says. She pauses and stares at him for a few moments longer. "You definitely have an athletic build. And you do look like you would be good at running. Also looks like you have some experience in battle."

Aaron wonders how she knows he has been in some battles. Does he look like a killer? Like he has murdered women and children without a second thought? Killed opposing men trying to protect their people and village?

Victoria suddenly grabs Aaron's upper forearm. He flinches, but doesn't move away. He forces himself not to jerk or make her loosen her grip on his arm. He can't see her as a threat. He needs to act normal.

Victoria traces the only noticeable scar on Aaron's arm, from the crook of his elbow to the outside of his right wrist. The other scars look almost nonexistent. Victoria's finger traces it back and forth, softly and slowly.

"It must have been an intense battle a few years ago for a scar to look like this. It doesn't look like it was treated. It isn't as smooth as it can be. Was it infected?"

"I guess." Aaron can't tell her the truth. It would give away who he is and where he came from. Simon refuses to allow anyone to tend to a wound of any size.

"That isn't a confident yes or no."

"So?"

"Did it become infected?"

"I can't remember." Aaron tells himself it's alright to lie. She won't know. It's better to lie and survive than to be truthful and die. Or worse, be sent back. Or even worse, be forced to lead all of Revelation back and confront Simon.

"Follow me to the training area. You are going to perform some different tests and I'm going to track your progress. After that, we are going to head to the classroom and I'm going to see how you place mentally. Once we finish both sets of tests, I will compile everything and see how you compare to everyone else in the compound. How you score compared to others will determine if you plan our attacks or participate in them. Understand?" Victoria speaks quickly, as if she barely has to think about what she is saying. Aaron struggles to catch every word, but he just doesn't understand it all. Is compiled a word? What is a classroom? Do people really plan attacks? Aren't they just started whenever the leader feels like attacking someone? Various questions run through Aaron's mind. He can't understand anything.

Maybe that is how Simon operates, not planning his attacks. That wouldn't surprise Aaron. Is that why no one beats Simon? If he randomly attacks, that means the enemy has no time to prepare. Is that his secret? Is that why Aaron really never knew when he was going to have his next training session?

Aaron wishes he isn't so stupid. He would be able to form an actual question so he could ask what certain words meant. If he wasn't this stupid, he would know what all these words meant. He knows what mental means. Is she going to see how stupid he is in this classroom? If so, he wants to leave. He wants to just do the physical part and then run away. He doesn't want Victoria to know he is too stupid to function normally.

"Yeah." Aaron says.

"Good! Now follow me. I doubt anyone bothered to show you around. I'll give you a quick tour. Probably a week, you won't be having any free time. You will either be planning or training. I think you are going to get placed into training, but I still have to give you both tests. If you are in training you will be working your body to make it stronger and learning to fight with all the different weapons we have. You will only have breaks to go to the bathroom, eat, shower, and sleep. Your sole focus will be preparing your body to withstand battle. If you are in planning, you will spend all your time gathering information about not only Revelation but also retrieving information our people and our allies bring back to us about anything that can be considered helpful to us in our future battles." Victoria talks steadily, as if she has given this speech several times before.

As she leads Aaron out the door and down the hallway, he notices all emotion is gone from her voice. He must keep up with Victoria. He knows he will get turned around if he falls behind. She walks extremely quickly down the hall. Most would have to run to keep up with her, but Aaron nonchalantly follows. He is glad he has his speed. It makes it easier to get around when someone is walking so quickly in her domain. As they walk, he tries to figure out why she sounds so distant. It is as if she would rather do anything else other than giving her little speech.

"We just left Clayton's library. The room is connected to his office. Never go see him unless you are invited personally or escorted by me."

The two walk down the hallway for a few seconds before Victoria talks again.

"The entire compound is connected by this one hallway. Doors may open up to other hallways or just another room. This main hallway makes it easier for everyone to walk from one side of the compound to the other. The various doors we are passing are to someone's room or supplies."

Aaron nods and continues to follow her.

"This is the cafeteria. It's in the center of the compound,

making it easy for everyone to find it. The bathroom is here as well. Plumbing is sparse around here. Other than Clayton's room, this is the only other place with a toilet in the compound.

"Everything to the left of the cafeteria, from where I am standing facing north, is bedrooms, supplies, the main entry, and Clayton's office. Everything to the right is planning and training. Follow me and we'll head to the training room. After that we will head back to take the test and then I will take you to your bedroom."

The two walk towards the east, leaving and taking a right out
of the cafeteria. Aaron doesn't say much and neither does Victoria. She quickly stops after walking for a few minutes.

"This is the Brains area. They plan and study here. Now we are going to head to training."

Aaron looks at her eyes. He knows how to read a person. He might not be able to put what she is feeling into words, but he can see sadness in her eyes. He can see she is mechanically telling him where the cafeteria is, but her mind is thousands of miles away, reliving a sad moment or revisiting a bad memory. He feels an odd sensation inside of him. He has never felt this before after looking at someone who is sad, but he wants to put his arm around her shoulder. He isn't sure why.

Whenever Aaron is down, Jonathan would put his arm around Aaron. Aaron knows that it is the proper gesture to try to make someone feel better. He has never felt the urge to do it before. Normally he enjoys seeing a person suffer. Why does seeing her sad pull at his heart strings?

"Okay," Aaron says to her.

The rest of their walk is in silence. It's only another three minutes, but it's slow and filled with questions running through Aaron's mind. How does he manage to have so many questions but not be able to hold conversations and form sentences like everyone else?

When they arrive, Victoria says nothing and opens the door.
She doesn't hold it open for Aaron to enter. That doesn't bother him. He is sure some would be bothered by it, but he is used to having to enter and exit places on his own. He has never had help.

"Okay, time to begin. Notice this is a really big training area. We won't be doing everything in here, but most of it. I chose now to do these tests because all the trainers are out in a mock battle, preparing for one next week, and I figured you would like some privacy. Almost all the new kids do." Victoria starts to walk down towards the end of room. She walks around three hundred feet straight until she stops just before the wall.

"Alright! You are going to run as quickly as possible from where you are standing to here. When I shout go, you start running!" Victoria shouts as loudly as she can.

"Ready? Set!" Aaron isn't sure what she is saying. Isn't she just supposed to say go so he can start running?

"Go!" Victoria shouts the key word as Aaron is thinking.

He starts running towards her after a second of hesitation. He is still wondering what she is doing. Why say two unnecessary words before saying the key word? He feels extremely sluggish. He knows he can run quicker than this. Maybe his times won't stick out as abnormal.

"Good. Now I want you to run the perimeter of this room ten times in a row. Ready? Go!" Victoria tells him to do this as if it's simple to her.

What is a perimeter? He starts to run straight, but isn't sure what to do. He just runs until he almost runs in the wall.

"Stick to the walls but don't run into them!"

He does what she says and follows the walls. Walking to Reformation is more boring than running in a circle, but running around the room ten times is more boring than tiring. He has run for ten hours straight before and barely broke a sweat. After Simon's training, anything that is considered to be difficult is easy for him.

He looks like he has only run half of a half mile when he finishes all ten laps. Victoria looks at him with a weird face, but shakes it off and moves on.

She walks over to some weights and motions for Aaron to follow her. He walks over, looking as if he has been standing for hours on end and has done nothing.

"Okay, lift as much as you can. I'll add the weight." Aaron has never lifted actual weights before. Heavy rocks, yes; actual weights that need proper form, no. He isn't quite sure what to do, but he maneuvers his body under the bar. He has seen guys at Revelation have the luxury of training with real equipment and not lift rocks like Aaron. Since it is a luxury at Revelation, they are normally the ones who die first in battle.

He lifts the bar without any weights on it, and winds up nearly throwing it. It is so light!

"Weight." Aaron doesn't try to form a fancy sentence. He knows Victoria will understand. She adds some weight and he lifts again. It's still too light for him.

"More." She adds more than she did last time. Once again, he lifts. He can't easily throw it, but it's still too light.

"More." Victoria groans and adds more than she did before. Aaron wants to chuckle at her for being lazy, but he chooses not to. That might make her mad. He lifts the bar one last time. He can still lift more, but if he held this for a while he would definitely have sore arms. He puts the bar down and maneuvers out from under it.

"Good job. Most of the new guys don't even know how to lift. Now you will lift with the dumbbells and then we are done here. Everyone will be coming back in a few minutes, but I've seen all I need to see. After the dumbbells we will head over to the classroom."

Aaron doesn't want to go to the classroom. What did Victoria see? Did he perform too well? Did he give away that he is Simon's weapon? Aaron rushes through the dumbbell exercise. It isn't any different from the weight bar. It's lifting two smaller bars instead of one bar.

"Good job. Now walk with me to the testing room for the second part of your assessment." Victoria quickly runs out of the room. Aaron has to briskly jog to keep her in sight so he doesn't lose her and become lost. They don't go far before Victoria ducks into a room and actually holds the door open for

Aaron to walk in.

"Alright, this test is written with no time limit, so take your time. I'm going to hunt down Clayton and drag him down here so we can place you today and not make you wait. Good luck!" She runs out of the room and slams the door behind her. Great. Now Aaron is alone. He is about to prove he is the stupidest person on the planet.

He sits down at the only table with a piece of paper on it. There is a pencil next to it. He isn't prepared for this. He looks at the first question, then the second, and the third. He doesn't know how to answer any of them. There are only three questions total.

1. Imagine you are stranded from your team during battle. What would you do to survive?

2. You have been stabbed in the stomach and are bleeding to death. Your friend has been stabbed in the chest. You know you will not survive if you make it back the compound. You don't know if your friend has any chance of living. Do you choose to lay there and die, or do you make it your last mission to deliver your friend to the compound so he can have a chance to live?

3. What is the best way to take down Revelation?

He sits there and thinks. His handwriting is notorious. He taught himself the best he could. He taught himself how to read. At least this isn't a verbal test. He would fail. Never being taught to speak is a benefit to Simon, but a downfall for Aaron if he were to escape. Aaron can never tell anyone anything, but he also can't explain himself to anyone. Maybe that is why Simon never allowed anyone to teach Aaron to speak or what words meant. Aaron always has to teach himself to figure out what people are saying.

He picks up the pencil and starts to write. He writes the truth. He writes what he knows will help him survive. If he were stranded, he would run back to the compound, away from the battle. If he were dying, he would enjoy his death. He has always wanted to die. Why waste the one thing he has looked forward to for the past fifteen years to take someone back to the compound that might die anyway? The best way to take down Revelation is from the inside, picking off Simon's right hand men, and then taking down Simon when he least expects it.

He doesn't add anything. He puts his raw answers down on the paper. He doesn't worry about making perfect sense. Victoria and Clayton will have a good idea of what he is saying.

As he finishes writing both Clayton and Victoria walk into the room. Clayton angrily takes Aaron's paper and crumbles it into a ball and throws it. He isn't mad at Aaron. Aaron can tell something else ticked off Clayton.

"You performed the slightest bit better than all the other trainers," Clayton states in a monotone yet angry voice.

Victoria sighs and looks at Aaron.

"You did fine. I shouldn't have given you the mental test. Sorry." Victoria looks down at the floor with a frown on her face.

"It's fine." Aaron allows no emotions to enter into his voice. He
is glad neither of them read the paper. The blunt truth isn't something he should reveal yet. What if they don't know about Simon being the ringleader? If they don't, he would have given away that he is a weapon, a weapon of mass destruction.

"Tomorrow, you begin training. Good luck. Victoria, take Aaron to his room. Then go to bed yourself. It's late. You both need sleep." Clayton speaks as if he is talking to children. Victoria motions for Aaron to follow. Aaron slowly stands. Relief washes over him. He made it through the first day without giving himself away. That's an accomplishment.

As Victoria and Aaron exit, Clayton waits and then picks up the paper he crumbled. He decides not to open it and read it. Something in the back of his mind tells him to keep it. Clayton isn't sure what it is about Aaron, but he knows there is something about Aaron that he can use to his advantage.

6 Training

Aaron is supposed to be sleeping, but he can't stop thinking. He is filled with questions he wants answered. He knows he can't ask. There are no answers. Only Simon can answer the questions Aaron has. Even if Aaron can manage to lock Simon in a room, Simon would never explain anything to Aaron.

The sound of rain fills Aaron's ears. Thunder quickly follows, with cracks of lightning. As he would in Revelation, he needs to see the storm.

Reformation has given Aaron a fully stocked room. He has a bed with sheets, multiple pillows, and a heavy blanket, or, as Victoria calls it, a comforter. He has a large closet, filled with everything he could need. It's stocked with basic tee shirts, mainly white, gray, and black, but a few shirts have images on them. Victoria says they are from the world before now. Aaron has no idea what Victoria means by that statement. He also has a variety of dark blue and black denim, multiple jackets, and also a few pairs of shoes and boots.

Why does he have all of this? Maybe this is why Reformations always loses. Luxuries are for the weak. No one needs this much. Or do they? Is this normal? Is Simon wrong? Or are Victoria and Clayton?

Questions plague Aaron's mind as he randomly grabs a jacket and puts it on. He feels extremely warm. It's an odd sensation, but it feels good. He has never felt this before. The only time he feels extremely warm is in a room with no windows, or when he is outside. For some reason, he feels comfortable. He actually likes it. He might wear it more often.

Thunder cracks again. He can hear a tree slowly snap and fall to the ground. If it hits twice, flames will begin to dance.

He crawls out of his window. It is the fastest way to the roof. He can jump or climb up there easily. He can find his way onto the roof. And he does. There is an air conditioner unit right outside his room. It is no longer in use, but it makes the jump a little shorter and strains his body less. He has become used to fewer aches and pains. He is enjoying this small amount of time with no pain.

When he reaches the roof, he is already soaked. The rain is pouring harder than in more recent storms. It hurts a little, as if the raindrops can leave welts. Aaron doesn't look around much. There is no cover anywhere on the roof. He will have to sit out in the rain.

Aaron shivers from the memory. Simon is watching the training carefully today. Aaron isn't able to remember why, but that is not important. He is twelve and has been training for two hours now. He is exhausted. The beating is rough, painful, and never-ending. Normally he would just sit there and take it, but today he isn't in the mood.

Instead of being a good little punching bag, he stares down one of the puppets. He starts mumbling under his breath, describing the pain of having acid thrown onto bare skin. The first puppet is taken over by intense pain. The second puppet he stares down he decides to give the feeling of the pain of being whipped by a burning chain. Both puppets are rendered helpless.

In an intense moment of anger, Aaron snaps both of their necks. Aaron looks at Simon and is ready to make Simon feel extreme pain and kill Simon as well. Aaron is then taken down by stronger puppets within seconds of killing the two puppets.

When Aaron comes to, he is chained by his neck, naked, outside, alone, during a horrible storm.

He is left out there for a week with no food, water, clothing, or protection of any kind.

Three, four, and five streaks of lightning fill the night sky. Thunder booms dangerously. The storm is incredibly intense. Due to the noise of the thunder, Aaron has yet to hear another person running along the roof top. If he had, he would have tracked the person's movements until he decided whether the person was an enemy.

The storm doesn't last long. This is an extremely rare occurrence. Normally, the storms last for hours on end, beginning when the sun sets and continuing until it rises again. Aaron sits on the roof until he decides to look for a way to descend to solid ground.

Suddenly, whoever managed to stay hidden for a full hour mistakenly kicks a single bolt that must have been loosened and knocked off during the storm? Aaron's ears pick up the sound, so insignificant and quiet but loud enough for him to hear. He immediately turns his entire body in the direction the sound came from. He hones in on the person, focusing only on the possible enemy.

Aaron doesn't move and neither does the enemy. The surrounding darkness makes it difficult for Aaron to make out who is standing before him. His eye sight is better than anyone's, almost like an animal's, needing less light than an ordinary human to make out objects, but even he needs more to see his enemy. Aaron takes a step. The enemy begins to run to Aaron's right. He takes off immediately. He sprints and appears in front of the enemy within half a second. If the enemy is from Reformation, casually gazing at the storm like Aaron, he can't just scare or show whomever it is that he isn't normal. He is still fast and catches up. He grabs the left shoulder and turns the person around roughly.

"Oh! Aaron, you scared me! I thought you were a rouge coming to kill us. Why are you up here?" Victoria asks.

He wasn't expecting her to be on the roof, much less

during one of the worst storms Aaron has ever had the pleasure of watching. She looks too delicate to be out here. She is barely tall enough to rest her head on Aaron's shoulders, and he could snap her in two if she were in his path while he was outraged and beginning a killing spree.

"The storm." He doesn't feel the need to even try to formulate a sentence. He hopes to avoid the embarrassment.

"Can I ever expect a real sentence from you?" She asks, annoyance working its way into her voice.

"No." With his response, Victoria laughs and removes Aaron's hand from her shoulder.

"You're such a weirdo. We should go in and sleep. You have training in three or four hours."

Victoria turns her back to Aaron and leaves. She lifts a panel from the roof and exposes the inside of Reformation. She jumps down. Aaron knows it isn't a far drop, maybe ten feet. Victoria doesn't close the panel. She leaves it open, as if she expects Aaron to follow her.

"Coming?" Victoria shouts from the floor below. Aaron reluctantly follows. He wants to stay on the roof until training starts, but with Victoria it looks like he isn't having his way.

"There you are! Off to bed, now mister!"

It's not like Aaron isn't used to orders, but he wants to know why Victoria is ordering him around. Victoria escorts his room, watches to ensure he enters and lays down, and then leaves him to fall asleep. But he cannot make himself sleep.

He lays awake until morning comes and he hears movement outside. He jumps up and exits his room. Stares, evil eyes, glares, hatred filled the hallway. He doesn't understand why, but then he knows why. He is new. New people are never liked. They know nothing, they act differently, they see the world differently. Aaron remembers all the glares the new puppets receive from the older puppets. Human nature never changes.

He slips back into his room and closes the door. It doesn't take long before movement ceases outside his door. He peeks his head back out into the hallway when the coast is clear. He steps out of his room and closes the door. His stomach growls.

He follows his nose, trusting his sense of smell better than his memory of the compound. He finds the cafeteria. He spots Victoria. She is surrounded by males who are shoveling yellow mashed up bits into their mouth. He doesn't dare go over and address her. He knows he shouldn't intrude.

He walks over to a line of people and stands in it. Those who are in the front are taking food out on trays. He moves when the line moves and thinks little of the situation. Then it hits him. He doesn't know what any of the food is called.

"Aaron! Aaron! Aaron!" A female voice calls his name over and over again. He looks to his left and there is Victoria, flailing her arms. He looks at her questionably and she sprints over to him.

"What?" He is blunt, but not rude.

"Let me help you order. It's sort of weird around here. Plus, you don't have your meal card yet. Can't receive food without it!" She hands him a small card with the word soldier artfully written. He holds it, but never looks at it.

"Thanks."

"No problem. Hey Jeremy!" Victoria turns her attention to the cook. Aaron didn't even notice he was so close to receiving his food. "Okay, so here's the deal. Brains and Soldiers receive different meal plans. We want everyone here to be healthy and have all the nutrients they need, but food is being charged at ridiculously high prices. We have to limit everything. Since you are a Soldier, you will have a high protein and antioxidant diet. You will have some sort of meat on your plate with a green vegetable three times a week. The other four times you will have greens and fruit with a small amount of fish. At every meal you will have a large glass of water. You will have two meals a day."

"Okay."

"Show them this card and they will give you the appropriate food. Hopefully you aren't picky with your food, because there are no choices here." Victoria points her hand towards Jeremy.

"Okay." Aaron says as he hands his card to the cook.

"Jeez, Victoria, talk a little more, why don't you!" Jeremy's sarcasm is rude, and Aaron doesn't like it. Why is he being mean to Victoria? She deserves better.

"Oh just give him his food Jeremy!" Victoria snaps, not seeming to take the words to heart.

"So bossy. Maybe he isn't hungry." Jeremy starts to prepare the food for Aaron on a plate.

"Oh, by the way, Aaron, there are only certain times

when you can eat food. If you miss it, you miss it. Now eat quickly! I am leading your training today. Normally you would work with your other fellow Soldiers, but it takes a little while for everyone to adjust, and I like to personally make sure all the new kids learn the most effective way to train."

Jeremy looks as if he has heard this speech a hundred times and gives Aaron his food. Aaron and Victoria walk over to a table and sit down so Aaron can eat. He tastes nothing as he shoves it in his mouth. He bites mechanically, chews, and swallows. He doesn't need to experience the flavor. Experiencing food entering his body is incredible.

The second Aaron finishes, Victoria jumps from her seat and leaves. Aaron follows her to the training area. All of the Soldiers are training in various ways. Some are lifting weights, others are running, some are sparring, a few are using weapons.

"Ever used a weapon before?" Victoria asks Aaron.

"No," he replies.

"Show me what natural talent you have then. Pick up that sword about ten feet to your left. See if you can hit me. Trust me, you can't hurt me, so don't be afraid to use force." Aaron grabs the sword. It looks very old. It's long, thin, and shiny. Victoria picks up a large, fat, long stick. Aaron immediately thinks this is going to end just as it did with the puppets in Revelation, her beating him and him near death on the floor.

Suddenly, Victoria hits him. It hurts really badly. Why does he think she is fragile?

He tries to strike her with the sword. He has no idea how to function with this giant sharp metal. He moves it awkwardly and has no chance of hitting her. He is incredibly slow with wielding the weapon and she is hitting him left and right. He eventually gives up trying to hit Victoria and focus on not being hit.

Victoria continues to hit him. Aaron is attempting to avoid her hits, but he is not doing well. He isn't used to fighting in close combat. Long distance is his preferred fighting style. Eventually, Victoria becomes tired of beating Aaron.

"Well, you have no natural talent in using a sword. I am not going to even try to have you move with a dagger or ninja stars. How well can you use a bow and arrow?"

They walk to the other end of the training area. Aaron receives a variety of odd looks from others in the room. He doesn't like it. He should be used to strange looks by now. Back at Revelation, a successful experiment is a rare thing that many puppets can't understand. The puppets don't think it's possible for anyone or
anything to exit Simon's basement alive, much less three times.

"Pick up the bow, grab an arrow, and shoot." Victoria points at the bow while looking at Aaron.

The instructions seem clear. He does what he is told. He knows this isn't going to work. He has no idea how to hold the bow, add the arrow, or do anything. How does someone even aim at the target with this contraption?

Victoria stands to the side giggling. She enjoys watching

him squirm. He keeps trying to hold the bow differently, trying to find a comfortable way to hold it, but it just isn't working.

"Want some help?" Victoria asks Aaron softly after a few minutes.

"No." Aaron continues to try to hold the bow differently.

"Are you sure?" Victoria prompts the question immediately after Aaron begins to try to hold it upside down.

"Yes." Aaron answers harshly. Victoria says nothing for a while. Aaron almost forgets she is there.

"Want me to show you how to hold it?" Victoria tries to take the bow from Aaron as she asks her question.

"No." Aaron is more annoyed with himself than her questions. He wants to do something correctly, but she isn't helping him. He has to do this on his own to show her he isn't too stupid.

"Want me to shut up?" Aaron wants to say yes, but he doesn't want to offend her. She continues to hold her stick. She does have a powerful swing. He already has around ten or so bruises from her stupid stick. He decides not to say anything.

He finally has an idea of how to hold it. He probably isn't right, but he doesn't care if he is right at this point. He doesn't really need to know how to shoot a bow and arrow. He can send people into a world of pain with one look and then snap their neck when they can't handle the pain. He never has to try. He can always easily kill his opponents. He never needs to use a bow and arrow, sword, dagger, or any weapon during battle. He has no reason to learn how to use pointless weapons when he is a weapon.

He holds the bow with his left hand and uses his thumb to hold the head of the arrow. He pulls the string back with his right hand and holds the tail of the arrow with his right thumb. He thinks he has it right. The tension on the bow is intense. Is he going to break it? What if he does? Will someone beat him for it? He releases the string from the bow and the arrow from his right hand.

The arrow travels maybe five feet in front of him. Victoria laughs. Aaron puts his head down in shame. He clearly does not know how to use a bow and arrow. After this experience, he doesn't want to know how. He would love to snap the bow in half and walk away right now.

Aaron tries to shoot the arrow again, but ends with the same result. For the next hour, he continues to attempt to shoot. Victoria doesn't move. Instead she watches him.

Aaron spends another hour trying to learn how to shoot the bow and arrow. He counts three hundred arrows that he has shot.

Victoria has sat down at some point. Aaron wonders why she hasn't left.

"How about you give up? There's always tomorrow. You can't learn everything in one day."

She stands and begins to stretch. Aaron continues to shoot until she puts her hand on his right shoulder."

"Come on. We both need showers. Try again in the morning." Victoria quickly takes the bow out of his hands and lays it down.

Without a word, she turns around and begins to walk

out. Aaron jogs towards her. He is determined to master the bow and arrows as soon as he can, with or without Victoria watching.

7 Discovery

No one speaks to him, even after a month; they refuse to acknowledge his existence. He is just a new person, nothing special. He has no special abilities, or so they think. He wishes he could show them. Constantly hearing words under their breath about his mediocre performance makes him angrier than he has ever felt before. If only Aaron could throw one of them up against the wall and cause him to feel like he would rather be dead than feel another ounce of pain from Aaron. The thought of it actually excites him. Aaron might not be able to use weapons as efficiently as everyone else, but why should he? He is capable of killing fifty people compared to the number that they can kill with the weapons they use.

As Aaron mechanically swallows, he fights the urge to puke. He may not have been able to enjoy food daily while living under Simon's eye, but now he wishes he isn't forced to eat the gross, tasteless mass Reformation calls food. He feels alone at the table, even though he is surrounded by people in the compound.

Aaron forces the last bite in his mouth. He shivers. This feels like a form of torture. Is it really possible for a substance to be both slimy and hard, especially if it is meant to be consumed and digested? Aaron rises to leave, throwing his tray in the overwhelming stack. Murmurs of disproval of the food come up behind him.

He knows he isn't meant to engage in the conversation behind him. He knows he could add something to it, but he knows he can't. He could agree with the two men behind him and describe how the food feels like a lizard crawling down his throat, rough but soft. He can't form the words needed to join their conversation. It's not like they want him in there anyway. He is just there. That's all. He doesn't do anything spectacular or anything. He can't do anything to match anyone else's abilities. If Aaron wasn't there, Reformation would run just fine.

He quickly walks from the room. He looks around. He doesn't see anyone. Is it safe to run? He does anyway. He sprints to the training area. He has memorized the path so he can run there and back quickly. Aaron isn't fond of walking at a normal pace with everyone. He prefers to sprint to training in twenty seconds.

He arrives, barely winded from the run. He misses training at Revelation. He didn't have to hide who he is. However, he was beaten, whipped, burned, strangled, doused in acid, lit on fire, tortured daily.

Aaron is glad he is now at Reformation. The worst ache he has here is muscle aches. He doesn't have to worry about being beat so badly he might die. But he can't act naturally during training. It really is bothersome to keep worrying about being noticed.

No one is in the training area. Aaron walks over to the weights. He needs to reach his limit today before anyone else comes in. Lifting a little over one hundred pounds isn't helping him. He has lifted boulders in the past. He knows he can lift a measly one hundred.

He adds weight to the bar. He makes it two hundred. He has no reason to cause himself unnecessary injury. Aaron knows it's better to start lighter and then add weight instead of trying to dead lift too much weight. He pushes the bar up. He can lift more. He adds another one hundred. He lifts again. He has the same reaction. He adds fifty more. Three hundred fifty pounds challenges him.

He enjoys the slight shaking of his arms as he lowers the weight to his chest. He lifts the bar fifty times. A slight chime like the sound of metal hitting metal makes Aaron stop. He puts the bar back in its original position and sits up. He looks around, trying to figure out what could have made the sound.

He brushes if off. It could have been something he did. It doesn't matter. No one is around, so he hasn't given himself away. He racks the weights in their proper places. He doesn't need anyone walking in and seeing a weight bar with three hundred fifty pounds on it.

He walks casually over to the bows and arrows. The first day, he couldn't shoot the arrow. Aaron was determined after that day to master the bow. He came every night for two weeks to be able to successfully shoot arrows at a target. Now he has to act like he has progressed normally. He has to act like he still can't shoot the arrow. He hates it. Being himself would be so much easier.

He grabs a bow and an arrow. He aims for the target. He shoots a perfect bull's eye on his first try. He is used to having to master things as quickly as possible. He can't understand how these people can't pick up new skills quickly. Then he remembers none of
them are experiments, created to be a weapon.

He shakes his head. He can't let this bother him. After nineteen years, this shouldn't bother him. Why does it now? Why does knowing he is different bother him now? Is it because he is around normal people? Or is it because he has seen the kindness of others?

He shoots a few more arrows. Every time they hit the center of the target dead on. This is too easy for him. He sets down the bow and grabs a dagger. He throws it with no effort. Like the arrows, it is dead on in the center. He shakes his head. This isn't difficult for him. Acting like he can't is.

He goes around and removes all of the arrows and the dagger from the targets. Just as he removes the last one, a giant mass of Soldiers walks in. They all enter at the same time, but disperse to the different types of training quickly. No one comes near Aaron. Wherever he is standing or training, they will avoid that area completely.

He shakes his head and throws what he has collected down. He doesn't care. He heads towards the door. He is done with training for the day. He has nothing new to do, and he isn't in the mood to fake it. As he exits, he notices Victoria sprinting down the hallway. Aaron takes no time in deciding to follow her. He runs after her, quietly.

Although Aaron has lived at Reformation for a month, he has yet to explore. He is afraid he will go somewhere he shouldn't. All the winding halls, unmarked doors, and confusing room placements make it difficult for Aaron to convince himself to explore.

Aaron wonders how anyone gains the confidence to walk through these halls as he follows Victoria. She isn't walking slowly, but this isn't the pace Aaron would walk if he were in a hurry. Then again, no one can reach that speed if a person hasn't been mutated in a laboratory. Aaron is annoyed that Victoria is walking so slowly. He wishes she would go faster.

Suddenly, she stops, opens a door, and walks in, slamming the door shut behind her.

Aaron has no idea where he is or how to go back. Simon is right. Aaron lacks the ability to think things through. If he had the ability, he wouldn't be in this situation.

Behind the door, something heavy and fragile falls and breaks. Or is it thrown? Aaron presses his ear to the door. His hearing can pick up the tiniest of sounds. It sounds as if someone is arguing far away from the door, on the other side of the room. He wants to hear what is being said. He knows Victoria is behind the door, he knows she is talking, but he needs to know what she is saying.

The sounds move closer to the door. Aaron has nowhere to run, hide, or avoid what is about to happen. Whoever is in there is about to come out, see Aaron, and think he is hunting for information.

As the sounds come closer, Aaron can start to hear them. He hears his name. Now he really wants to know what is being said. He is so close to hearing. Then the sounds stop right in front of the door. Aaron can hear every word.

"I know what I saw!" Victoria sounds distraught and annoyed. Aaron has only ever heard her happy and distant. Now she is determined to be understood.

"Victoria." Aaron recognizes the male voice. He has heard it once or twice before. He can't put a name to the voice. It is male, a little older and deeper than Aaron's own voice. It has a gentle, caring tone.

It reminds Aaron of Jonathan. Jonathan used the same tone when Aaron needed to be comforted after a difficult training when he was younger. Aaron wonders how Jonathan is. He violently shakes his head. He can't think about Jonathan right now. He must know why his name is mentioned.

"No! Don't Victoria me."

"I'm not sure you saw what you think you saw."

"Clayton, I know what I saw." That's where Aaron heard that voice before. A month ago he was introduced to Clayton. What could Victoria have seen Aaron doing that would make her go to Clayton?

"Tell me what you saw. If you tell me calmly you are less likely to exaggerate."

"I was cleaning the upper level of the training room. It's my normal morning routine. Aaron came in early. I thought it was good for him to show he is serious about training to take out Revelation. He can run well, but last time I saw him, he couldn't do anything but run.

"He went over to the bench. I know he can lift the same as the other guys, so I don't know why I looked. For some reason, I watched him. Clayton, he lifted at least three hundred pounds! I don't know anyone that can lift that much. Afterwards, he went over and shot arrows. A month ago, he couldn't hold one. Today, every single one is a bull's eye. Isn't that a little strange to you?"

Aaron backs away from the door and leans against the wall opposite of the door. His heart slams against his ribs and stops working. She saw him. She gave him away. He isn't normal. Everyone is going to know. He is done. He is a freak. No one is going to want him around.

Aaron's life is over. He has no chance of being normal. He has been exposed. Victoria knows, Clayton knows, soon everyone will know. Should he leave? Should he run? Reformation is no place for him to be anymore.

The door opens, revealing Victoria and Clayton standing and talking.

"See you later. Next time don't rush me out!"

"I have better things to deal with Victoria." Clayton rolls

his eyes as he talks, pushing her out the door.

"Aaron?" He looks at Victoria, hiding all emotion from his face.

"You left quickly."

"Oh, I just needed to talk to Clayton."

"Everything good?" Over the past month, Aaron has found he can understand things a little better, but not much more than when he first arrived. His speech sounds slightly normal, but he still can't speak normally. He is hoping to sound normal.

"Yeah, thanks. Do you know where everything is yet?"

"No." Clayton chuckles at Aaron's remark.

"Victoria, teach him where all the rooms are. Aaron, learn the hallways. It's been a month and we can't baby you forever. Eventually we are going to attack. If you can't figure your way around here, how will you manage to find your way through the forest?"

Aaron wants to explain to Clayton he knows those woods better than Clayton, and he still knows almost nothing. Clayton doesn't know a thing about those woods, and that means all of Reformation knows even less. Simon would never allow any information about the compound's location or the surrounding woods to slip out. The mystery of Simon and Revelation is the only upper hand Simon has. Aaron holds his tongue.

"Yes sir." Aaron's answer is curt. In Revelation, Simon would have punched him for his tone of voice.

"Alright Aaron, come with me." Victoria walks away

from Clayton. Clayton is glaring at Aaron. Aaron isn't afraid of Clayton. No one can be as threatening as Simon. "Don't feel bad, it took me a couple months to find my way around. Let me give you some pointers about each of the hallways." Victoria starts to walk down the hallway, and Aaron follows. All the while, Aaron wishes he knew what both Victoria and Clayton were thinking. Why couldn't Simon have given Aaron the ability to read minds too? He can kill people and run miles and lift giant boulders with no effort, but he can't force his way into a person's mind.

As Victoria and Aaron walk further down the hall, Clayton turns around and walks back into his office. He closes the door and stares at the window on the other end of the room. He walks slowly to the window and looks at the woods.

After several minutes, he turns around and sits in his chair. He picks up a picture of an older man and looks at it. A small tear runs down his face.

"Is Aaron the Warrior Weapon? Is he the answer to winning this war against Revelation?"

8 Exposed

Aaron works with peppers this morning. Clayton told him he needed to allow his body to relax after yesterday's training. Because of Clayton, Aaron is stuck on kitchen duty. It isn't as bad as Aaron thought it was going to be.

He chops the peppers into small pieces. He despises the taste and feeling the pepper leave him with. His tongue always burns after eating a small bite. Not even water can eliminate the burn.

As Aaron is cutting, an eyelash starts to irritate his eye. He stops what he is doing, drops the knife, and tries to get the eyelash. He touches his eye. Pain spreads through his eye. He tries to rub his eyes. He is only making it worse. It is still burning. He has felt worse, but feeling little to no pain for three months has made him soft.

His eyes start to water. He runs to the bathroom. Will

Revelation

water help? He isn't sure how he found the bathroom. He doesn't think twice about it. He walks to the sink, turns on the faucet, and starts to splash water on his eye.

The burning isn't stopping. He needs to take out the contact. The burning is sitting right underneath the contact. If he does he will expose himself. Who is he kidding? He is already in trouble.

Soap foams abundantly as Aaron vigorously scrubs his hands. The other male in the restroom gives Aaron an odd look, but Aaron doesn't look up. He refuses to look at anything but his hands. He feels exposed. He scrubs his hands until they turn red.

He rinses his hands thoroughly. He touches his eye again, trying to take out one contact. He wants to scream.

He looks into the mirror at his reflection. Why hadn't he thought his idea through? Why did he think bleaching his hair would be good? His hair is already short, but a little longer on top. Only the longer hair has some bleached tips left. Every other strand of hair is his natural jet black.

It is too painful. It feels like the first experiment. The first real pain he remembers.

He is four. He sees the big metal door. He wants to know what is behind it. He tries to open it. It is too heavy for a child to open. Simon comes up behind him to offer his help. He is too young and naïve to understand Simon isn't offering his help. Simon is leading him to the basement, a place Aaron will soon learn he never wants to go into again. Aaron runs down the stairs. There are so many new things to look at. Different shapes of glass with different colored water are stacked high in shelves. One glass stands out to him. It is blue with a glowing orange ball in it. He wants to play with the ball. He hasn't seen one in weeks.

 Simon suddenly picks him up and angrily straps him to a cold metal table. Aaron doesn't like the cold metal touching his back. He tries to ask Simon why he did that, but Simon acts like he can't hear Aaron. Aaron notices some men in the room. A bright light hangs right over his face. He can't make out anyone.

 Simon goes over to the blue water. He fills up a needle with the water. The orange ball also goes in the needle. Aaron wants to know how a ball can do that. Simon walks towards him, an evil grin taking over his face. The other men in the watching Simon and Aaron start moving toward Aaron. Aaron doesn't know why. He wants off the table.

 Simon stands over Aaron. Simon grabs Aaron's eyelid. He holds Aaron's eyelid open and stabs the needle into Aaron's eyes. Aaron screams so loudly that he isn't sure if he is still screaming or if it is his own echo. He wants to die. He passes out while Simon starts on the second eye.

 Aaron shudders and covers his face with his hands. He rips the contact out of his left eye and then his right. He splashes water roughly onto his face. He runs out of the bathroom. He needs to go to a dark place, alone, away from the world.

 He sprints to his room. He runs past five people. He is running too quickly for them to notice. He doesn't count how

Revelation

long it takes to run to his room. He slams his door shut. He doesn't care who hears. He goes to his closet and flings open the door. He slams it behind him and sits in the corner furthest from the door. He takes out his knife. He was supposed to give it back after dagger throwing training, but he chose not to. What if he needed to relieve this pain?

He cuts his left wrist slowly and deeply the first time, then a second time, and a third. After seven cuts, he starts lightly cutting randomly. The blood intrigues him. It's not like the others. When he kills, his victim's blood runs everywhere. When he bleeds, no matter how deep the wound, it slowly seeps out and quickly congeals.

He can hear Victoria shouting his name over and over again, a string of curses following. He must be late for something. He can't remember being told he had to be anywhere.

He goes to answer, but before he does, he strips off the shirt that is now covered in blood.

Victoria flings the door open.

"I am tired of waiting! What is that act you put on earlier, slamming doors and spending two hours in the bath—"

He quickly turns around, but at the same time moves his left arm from behind his back as quickly and naturally as possible. He grabs a black long sleeve shirt and throws it on. He faces away from Victoria, hoping he won't flash his wrist. He doesn't care if she sees, but he doesn't want to appear any more freakish than he already is.

He turns back around to look at Victoria, but she is

gone. The door to his room is left wide open. He finds it odd he didn't hear her exit. Normally she drags the back of her heels as she walks, making it easy to hear her coming and going, but not today. She must have quickly run out of the room. Why?

He shrugs it off, and walks out of his room. Everyone should be finishing training. He doesn't feel like listening to the loud bellows of the Soldiers. They talk and yell for at least an hour before they actually start preparing to sleep. He doesn't think he can handle it tonight and stay calm.

He walks towards the training room. He isn't worried about running into Soldiers. They walk around him and ignore his existence. But not tonight. They all stop as they see him coming and begin to mumble. He slows his steps. He can't understand why they would stop.

"It's him." One of the Soldiers in the front of the group speaks first.

"He really is a freak." The Soldier takes a few steps back, fear evident in his face.

"Hasn't he killed three villages in a day?" A younger Soldier, no older than fifteen, asks his fellow Soldiers.

"I think it was just one," an older Solider answers.

"He's dangerous." The Soldier in the very front of the group states in a monotone voice.

It hits him. He has exposed himself. Purple eyes, black hair, pale skin, the description everyone knows about Simon's Warrior Weapon. He shuts down inside. Tonight he will die.

Aaron tries to take a step back. His heart races inside his chest, slamming into his ribs, almost painfully. He feels like prey. It is the same feeling he had before every one of Simon's trainings. He knows his death will not be quick. He is the reason so many from Reformation died. He is the reason so many people have died in surrounding villages. He is the bringer of death in this world, and he has brought death upon himself.

"Kill him!" The Soldier who said Aaron was dangerous yells at the top of his lungs.

They all charge at him. The word stupid keeps running through his head. He could run, find the exit, sprint into the forest. It would be easier. He knows he deserves this. He has killed too many. How long has he been waiting to die? Now he can, just not peacefully.

One of the more muscular Soldiers grabs him. Running is now out of the question. He could break one of his arms, but others would stop him from breaking the second. He decides he will take the beating. It won't be his first, but it will finally be his last.

They take turns, some punching, others bringing out weapons. They bring out chains, chairs, pipes. They have yet to bring out sharp weapons. He knows they want to torture him.

Jonathan would be disappointed in him. Aaron had the chance for freedom, a new start, a new life, and he wasted it. Jonathan would have run as far away as possible. He wouldn't have stopped walking in the forest for years. Aaron quit after two months. Jonathan was always better than him when it comes to brains. Aaron always won when it came to strength. Jonathan should be the one in Reformation, not Aaron.

Jonathan would have known more about Revelation and could have helped Clayton, Victoria, and the Soldiers take Simon down. Now Aaron is being mercilessly killed by the Soldiers.

The pain is unbearable. He hasn't felt real pain in months. Now he is being reintroduced, just before he dies. A peaceful death would be too easy. He deserves this pain. He has hurt too many, spilled too much blood. He could kill them all now, but he refuses. He closes his eyes and keeps his mouth shut. He refuses to whimper. He wants them to have their satisfaction. A weak weapon would only make them laugh, not giving them the revenge they need.

One man brings out a bow and some arrows. Everyone clears the area, except the largest Soldier. The one with the bow comes close to Aaron. It is impossible for him to hit anything but Aaron. The man behind him is safe. Six arrows are shot into Aaron, two in his shoulders, in his knees, and his feet. He wants to groan, but he won't.

Another man brings out the daggers. Two are lodged in his forearm, and four are lodged into each of his thighs. His body burns. He would have been on the ground by now had the large Soldier not been holding him above the ground. Blackness creeps into the edge of his vision. Nothing they have done now will kill him. He has had his heart punctured by three ribs and not died. He hopes they will find something to kill him.

Someone slices his shirt down the center of his chest, purposefully cutting deeply enough to draw blood. Laughter fills the hall. Revenge brings out the sickest part of humans. Is revenge what drives Simon? Could that be what has taken over his heart and mind? It makes sense to Aaron. The experiments, the bloodlust, it could all be for revenge. What could possibly have happened to Simon to cause such anger to take over his entire being?

Burning hot metal is stabbed into him. He flinches, grits his teeth, but refuses to make a sound. Someone has heated needles. They are stabbing burning needles into his chest. He stops feeling them after the first ten. He doesn't bother to count how many they push into his body.

Their torture is slow, but effective. He is breathing a little harder, his heart is working harder, and his vision is slowly going. Everything is a blur now. A fuzzy black border joins the blurry vision he already has.

"He's tough." Whoever said Aaron is dangerous makes another statement.

"He gotta be, bein' Simon weapen 'n all." A thick southern accent fits the Soldier well. He has scars all over his face. He must need this revenge.

"Makes me wonder how much more he can take." The first Solider responds to the southern Soldier.

"Why don't we just kill him now? We shouldn't act the same as him. We shouldn't torture him. We should kill him." The young Soldier sounds sympathetic. He is so young compared to the others. Should he be here?

"He probably is enjoying this pain." The same Soldier who said he is tough and dangerous roughly grabs his chin. "You enjoying this? Is this satisfying to you?"

Aaron can't see who it is, but his voice sounds familiar.

"Jeremy, leave him alone!" That's why the voice sounds familiar. He was helping Jeremy in the kitchen earlier. Wait, that is another familiar voice. Who?

The muscular Soldier holding him releases him. He falls to his right side on the floor. His head is swimming in pain, his vision is going big and then small. His head pounds. His body aches. Yet, he still isn't dead.

"If any of you try to run, I will stab you. We all know how accurate my aim is." The voice belongs to a female. It sounds so kind after everything he has already heard. "Aaron." The girl squats down beside him and brushes the hair out of his eyes. He doesn't notice. Aaron has only talked to one girl while at Reformation. His head has stopped pounding as much. The sudden fall to the floor probably contributed to that. He can think a little. The girl in front of him must be Victoria.

"Who started this?" A voice from behind him booms. The voice is full of authority. He knows this voice. It's Clayton's.

He isn't used to not seeing well. Normally, he sees the tiniest of dust particles swim past him. His vision is beyond perfect, yet now he is experiencing something completely new.

"I will repeat myself only once. Who started this?" Clayton's voice rings through the halls, demanding an answer. Yet, no answer comes.

Aaron is lifted off the ground. His vision might not be able to tell him who picked him up, but he knows it isn't any of the Soldiers, and Victoria is too weak to lift him. It must be

Clayton, the leader, the one who should actually want Aaron dead.

Aaron doesn't try to understand. He closes his eyes and tries to fight the urge to follow where they are going. He is in no state to focus on the winding hallway.

Eventually, they stop and Aaron is set down on a soft bed. It is twice the size of his own. He sighs as he moves to a comfortable position. The comfort lasts only for a short period of time.

Victoria and Clayton work together to remove the weapons. This is the last of the pain Aaron needs for his body to reach its limit. He screams as the third dagger is removed from his thigh, and goes unconscious. Victoria has tears streaming down her face while Clayton has the tiniest smile.

Reformation has finally found their weapon against Revelation.

9 Interrogation

The blinking of a florescent light wakes Aaron. The constant change of light irritates him too much for him to continue to sleep. He wonders when his room had a blinking light. He doesn't remember. He tries to sit. His arms burn as he applies pressure to them. He groans and immediately falls back onto the bed.

Why does his body hurt and feel like it is on fire? He doesn't remember doing anything yesterday other than helping out in the kitchen. He looks to the left and sees a white door. His room doesn't have any white doors. To his right, he notices a wall of books. This isn't his room.

Aaron's head spins. He has never seen this room before. Why is he here? This luxurious and large bed is three times as big as his. He tries to sit again, but the pain is too much. What could have possibly happened yesterday to make his body ache

Revelation

so much?

A door directly in front of him opens quickly. Aaron can't lift his head high enough to see who it is. Two sets of distinct angry footsteps walk to either side of Aaron. He looks up. Victoria is on his left, confused and hurt, and Clayton is on his right, both angry and happy.

At this moment, Clayton reminds Aaron so much of Simon. Both are leaders of a large group. He fears them both, but would never tell either of them that. Aaron knows he can't give anyone any weapon against him if he wants to hide his identity in Reformation.

Aaron knows not to say a word. One of them will talk eventually. What could he have done? Did he make someone sick yesterday? Did he miss training from sleeping too much? Should he have just stayed asleep?

"Explain yourself." Clayton crosses his arm and speaks with authority.

"How could you lie to us?" Victoria interrupts Clayton, wanting an answer.

"Victoria, let me—" Clayton is cut off quickly.

"No! You let me talk." A single tear streams down Victoria's face.

"Are you the leader?" Clayton glares at her.

"Does it matter?" Victoria throws her hands up in the air as she speaks.

"I make the rules. Now be quiet and let me talk, Victoria."

"I don't follow them." Victoria turns towards Aaron and

glares.

"I'm going to confront him." Clayton touches Victoria's shoulder to move her out of the way.

"No!" Victoria throws Clayton's hand away from her. "You should have the moment you figured him out! You chose not to say a word."

"What?"

"You knew he wasn't normal. You knew that day I came to you saying he is advancing too far too fast and is lifting an incredible amount of weight."

"Let me explain."

"No!" Clayton is cut off again. "I had a hunch which is why I came to you, but you never did a thing! I bet you wanted this to happen." Victoria starts to cry, but quickly wipes away her tears.

"Are you done?" Clayton asks after a few moments of silence.

"No!" She screams.

"Too bad. Aaron, explain yourself."

"Clayton!" Victoria screams at the top of her lungs. Aaron tries to figure out what is wrong. Why can't he be smarter and know exactly what is being said and understand everything? Why is he stupid? Why can't he teach himself how to understand? He taught himself to write and read.

"Aaron." Victoria's voice is harsh. He looks at her, carefully turning his head to the left. His entire body aches. He wants the pain to stop. He doesn't know what he does, but he knows he is pathetic. He used to have the ability to take beatings for weeks and still function just fine. Now he can't even move after a little pain. He is pathetic.

"Yes?"

"Did you come from Revelation?"

Aaron's eyes widen. He has been exposed. On the outside, Aaron is perfectly calm. On the inside, he is crumbling. His heart quickens, his body pulses, his forehead heats, sweat begins to bead. He has been exposed. He exposed himself. His life is over. He is dead. How did he allow this happen?

It hits him. The kitchen yesterday, the jalapeños, all the memories from the previous day fill his head. The beating, the stabbing, the pain, the suffering. How is he not dead? They should have killed him! He looks at Victoria. He chooses not to look at Clayton, but wonders if the two spared him. Why would they? Shouldn't they want him dead?

"Aaron, answer the question, truthfully." Clayton gives up trying to lead the questioning.

"Yes." Aaron's voice is hoarse. It hurts to speak.

"Did you come here to destroy us?" Victoria is glaring as she speaks.

"No." Aaron doesn't hesitate to answer this.

"Then why?" Clayton is kinder with his words. They don't have an angry tone like Victoria's.

"Destroy Simon." Aaron answers after a moment of hesitation. Clayton's eyes light up.

"Who?" Victoria looks confused. Clayton reaches over to grab Aaron's right arm. He cringes and jerks away. He doesn't release a sound, but tears build in his eyes. Every part of him hurts.

"Sorry, didn't mean to hurt you." Clayton is eager for information. "Aaron, look at me. Who is Simon?"

"Same as you."

Victoria stands to the side confused.

"What do you mean?" Clayton asks eagerly.

"Revelation's leader."

Clayton freezes for a moment, and then slowly adjusts his gaze from Aaron to Victoria. Aaron can't see their facial expressions. Have they never heard of Simon?

"How long has he been their leader?" Victoria sounds slightly panicked. Aaron can't understand why.

"Since he changed me or earlier."

"Aaron, are you genuinely interested in destroying him?" Clayton sounds stern, but almost happy. Why is he happy?

"Yes."

"You know, you almost died. You have been asleep for a little over two weeks now." Victoria tells Aaron this new information as if it is yesterday's news. How could he have slept so long?

Did he really almost die? Yesterday, or two weeks ago, he had accepted death. Now he is questioning the fact he almost died. Why isn't he dead? Hasn't that been what he wanted all along? Isn't death the one thing he has look forward to? Aaron feels like he is almost afraid of it now, but why? Death is all he wanted at Revelation. He was ready to die for killing so many. Why does Victoria's statement shock him?

Revelation

"Two weeks?" Aaron whispers. He can't believe it.

"Yeah. I wasn't sure you'd wake up. Not sure if I'm glad you did or not." Victoria glares at him.

"Victoria!" Clayton snaps at her.

"Clayton, he needs to know. No one likes him, especially me."

"Victoria, I doubt he knew." He knows no one likes him. What does Clayton mean?

"Clayton, you can't tell me he didn't know he was taking an innocent life! You," Victoria directs her attention to Aaron, anger and frustration in her voice. "I hate you!"

Aaron wants to ask why, but he knows why. He is a killing machine. He takes life. He causes pain to so many. He is a machine, one that is to be manipulated by its master as he pleases.

"Aaron, do you know who you killed five years ago?" Victoria has tears in her eyes as she asks. She hasn't calmed down. He can tell. He feels horrible for hurting her.

"No."

"His name was Daryl. He was strong, sweet, fast, and loveable. We were supposed to have our wedding the week after the battle. We had waited six years. I begged him not to go, but he said it would be quick and easy. No one knew Revelation's Warrior Weapon would be there. He was your first fatality that day. You didn't even give him a chance to move. You killed him, right there."

Aaron doesn't know what to say.

"You know, you remind me so much of him. You both

never show emotion and you both know when something is wrong. I thought maybe I could have him back. Maybe you could be just enough to make me forget him. How could I think that way when you are the murderer that took him from me?"

Victoria runs out of the room. Aaron understands about half of what she said. The pain from his body can't amount to the pain he feels in his chest. Victoria is nice to him, and all along he had taken away her most important person. What he has done would be the equivalent of losing Jonathan. Aaron knows he wouldn't be calm around whoever killed Jonathan. Aaron would kill him and everyone around him until he couldn't move another inch.

"You know, I can't say I can forgive you for taking away my men. But I can say this. I don't doubt in my mind that you didn't have any other choice. You want to destroy Simon. I want to destroy Revelation. You are exactly what I need to accomplish my goal. If we work together Aaron, we can both have what we want. I can help you and you can help me." Clayton kneels next to Aaron and looks at him. Aaron understands what he is saying.

"Victoria?" Aaron wants to know if she will be okay.

"She'll be fine. She forgives easily. She knows you didn't have another choice. Understand that there will always be hate and resentment towards you, but it will be minimal if you are truly different than the killing machine this Simon tried to make you. Aaron, work with me and we can both destroy those who destroyed parts of us and everything around us." Clayton sends Aaron a small smile.

"Okay."

"Great! I bet you're stiff. I'm going to go run a tub of hot water for you to soak in. Don't worry about my bed. I want you to relax. When you are better, we will both work to accomplish our goals. I'll make sure everyone understands that if they touch you, they have to deal with me."

Clayton goes to the door on Aaron's left and leaves it open. Aaron can hear the water running. He can't believe everything went as smoothly as it did. They could have killed him, but they have a purpose for him, one that isn't as sadistic as Simon's.

Aaron lays and thinks until Clayton comes to help him. Aaron tries to walk on his own, but collapses and screams in pain when he tries to stand. Clayton carries him. Clayton's expression goes from happy to sorrowful. Clayton helps Aaron out of his clothes, then turns to leave.

"Clayton." Aaron wants Clayton to know he appreciates everything he has done. To do that, Aaron says two words that he never thought he would say. "Thank you."

10 Clayton

Two painful days pass. Pain crawls over Aaron's body, deep in his nerves and muscles. He misses not having pain, but he knows this is temporary. As the days progress he notices the pain weakening. He will be pain free soon enough.

Aaron lies on his back, staring through the skylight above at the night sky. He has never had this luxury before. He has never seen the sky so calm and peaceful. It can't compete with the sight of a storm, but it is nice to look at. He wishes he could just lay in peace forever. He knows he can't. Soon he will pay for all the time he spent following Simon's orders.

A light knocking can be heard through the door. It is soft and delicate, signaling that Victoria will be walking in approximately ten seconds from now. He doesn't move or even look up. He stays in the same position and stares at the sky.

"Hey," Victoria whispers as she enters and closes the

door gently. "How are you feeling?"

"Fine."

"Clayton wants to know if you are well enough to walk to his office."

Aaron quickly identifies all of his injuries. A normal person wouldn't be able to walk after being stabbed repeatedly in the legs. He can't even feel the cuts anymore. They are already starting to scar. Healing has never been a problem for him.

Sitting up and throwing his legs over the bed silently, Aaron stands from his comfortable position. He says nothing, but silently bids the night sky farewell. He is still in the same clothes he was attacked in. Most would be bothered, but Aaron came from a life where he might receive a new set of clothes once a year.

Victoria leads the way to Clayton's office. Aaron still hasn't learned the labyrinth of Reformation. The walk is silent, but surprisingly quick. Could the giant bedroom be Clayton's? That would make sense. The room Aaron is staying in is the nicest he has seen in the compound. The leader normally stays in the nicest room that is close to the office. Simon does. Aaron only knows this because he was called to Simon's room multiple times.

Victoria violently opens a door when Aaron isn't paying attention. Maybe he won't be finding Clayton's office any time soon. They enter together and then Victoria closes the door silently. Clayton is sitting in a large chair adjacent to a large bookshelf, reading from a large book. It isn't as large as it is thick.

"For the word of God is living and powerful, and sharper than any two-edged sword, piercing even to the division of soul and spirit, and of joints and marrow, and is a discerner of the thoughts and intents of the heart," Clayton reads from the book.

"You have to love Hebrews," Victoria smiles at Clayton. Aaron is confused, but that is normal. What is a word of God? And who is Hebrews? Are they important?

"Aaron, how much do you know about the world before now?" Clayton has yet to look up from the book.

"Nothing."

"Come sit. This is going to be a long story, but an important one. I'm not going to cover dates or years or anything, just the major events."

Aaron goes and sits next to Clayton. He sinks into the large plush chair. His body instantly relaxes. Victoria quietly sits down on the floor.

"About seventy years ago, the world ended. Well, not ended, but severely destroyed. I'm a man who is strong in my faith. Scientists have been trying to explain the end for years, but I know the reason. I believe it deep in my heart. The bible basically says a world without Jesus and a world with Satan will run out of time and be destroyed. Seventy years ago, a man of faith was rare and the rarity of these men was pathetic. God told us that the world would end when His children stopped having faith. He chose to destroy the world.

"Many were spared, the true believers, the rarities. All

Revelation

those who didn't believe were wiped off the face of the planet. God's rage can build but subsides to those who truly have hearts filled with love for God and Jesus. The lands He destroyed can never return to their previous state. They are truly wastelands."

Clayton closes his book and lays it on the table across from Aaron. He looks at Aaron intently. Aaron looks back, but is confused. He can barely understand a word Clayton is saying, but at the same time he understands it, and he doesn't know why. Aaron remembers Jonathan talking about God taking them to a better place one day, but he never understood. Aaron still can't understand, but he does to a point.

"Even in the group of true believers, false believers and true evil still sprout. Wherever there is God, there is Satan. It is a never ending war between the two. Satan comes to change the hearts of God's children and can succeed if the child succumbs to the evil. That is how Revelation was created, hatred stemming from the heart of a twisted man. I never knew whom to pray for, but now I do. A man named Simon."

Clayton stands and starts to pace. He doesn't walk far from Aaron, but in a small circle. He begins to talk with his hands. He talks to his feet, but his voice is no longer calm.

"I pray for his heart to be returned to God and turned away from Satan. I have prayed for twenty years. I prayed for him while I prayed for God to call me to do something for Him in my life. I prayed for him when God called my father to create Reformation to reform those who joined Revelation. I prayed for him when he killed for my father. I prayed for God to give me the strength to forgive and glorify Him and for Him to show me what I needed to do. I continued to pray for him when God called me to take my father's place. I prayed to God, asking if blood needed to be shed over this leader, and I feel he never gave me an answer. I pray to God every night for that man to find his way back into God's grace and mercy, but he keeps going farther and farther from God and closer to Satan!"

Aaron sits and watches Clayton in shock. Clayton is taking in short quick breaths. Aaron looks at Victoria and notices she has a worried look on her face.

"Aaron?" Clayton's back is to Aaron. His voice is low.

"Yes?" Aaron answers like he is talking Simon.

"Do you know the difference between right and wrong?" Clayton turns his head to the right, but not to look at Aaron.

"Clayton!" Victoria jumps from her sitting position and stands with her fists balled.

"Shut up Victoria. Answer the question, Aaron." The entire room is silent. Clayton's tone is exactly like Simon's. Aaron isn't sure what will happen next.

"Yes."

"Clayton, stop." Victoria's voice is full of concern. Aaron isn't sure if it is for him or Clayton.

"Shut up or leave." Clayton has a serious look on his face. He means what he says. Aaron knows Clayton won't take anything from Victoria today.

"Aaron, do you know how many you have killed intentionally?"

"No." Clayton turns around as Aaron answers. He frowns as he looks down at Aaron, who is still sitting.

Victoria crosses her arms. Aaron knows she wants to say something to Clayton, but won't. She knows her place. Aaron knows his. Clayton knows his. Clayton is superior to everyone in the compound. When he says shut up, he means it. Clayton is probably the only reason Aaron is alive.

"I can't tell you. You have wiped out many entire villages. Villages full of small children, innocent people, women, husbands, and elderly people. Easily hundreds in every village, maybe even thousands, all because of you. How many did you kill unintentionally, or can you not even guess?" His voice is calm, but Clayton has tears running down his face.

Aaron doesn't say anything. He knows he deserves to hear this.

"So many people, some your age even, trying to kill you so you would stop killing! Innocent children crying out to their parents, their dead parents, to come back so they could be protected from you! Babies, small crying newborns, with no chance and you slaughtered them all! You had no compassion!" Clayton yells as tears stream continuously down his face.

The words sting Aaron. He has never thought about what he has done. He has never thought of all the deaths of the innocents. It never occurred to him that some people don't need to die. Why did it take him so long?

"Clayton, that is enough!" Victoria walks over to Clayton, tears streaming down her face.

"Victoria, leave!" Clayton's scream echoes in the room.

"Why do you want to torture him more? How do you know he wanted to? What if he was forced?" Her angry whisper is barely audible, but loud enough for all three of them to hear.

"And how do you know he wasn't?" Anger is threaded into every word Clayton says. The words sting. Aaron wants to run away and escape what is being said.

"Well, Clayton, why don't you ask him?" Victoria flips around, her ponytail brushing Clayton's face as she walks away from him, disappointed.

Clayton turns to Aaron. Aaron looks down at his feet. He doesn't want to be in this room. He wants to be on a roof, looking up at the sky. Calm night or a lightning storm, either would be enough. The weather is calming to him. He can't stand hearing this anymore.

Victoria crosses her arms and glares at Clayton. Clayton is staring Aaron down. Aaron wonders if he is waiting for a response. If he is, Clayton won't be hearing one. Aaron knows he can't form the words he needs to explain. He can write alright and can read, but he can't turn his thoughts into words very well. He can't speak the words. He can't even explain why he can't. He can never tell Victoria or Clayton that he wants to talk to them, but he just can't.

"Aaron, did you want to? Or were you forced?" Clayton is calm again. Only a few tears remain on his face.

Aaron wants to explain. He wants to talk and sit in silence. But he can't explain.

Revelation

"Aaron."

"Clayton, stop." Victoria's tone is the same as before, full of concern and hurt.

"Victoria, you said ask. Now I am. Aaron, answer me." Clayton walks right in front of Aaron and peers down at him. He is demanding an answer.

"Clayton, he isn't going to." Victoria seems to be helping, but Aaron can't see either of them caring about him. She knew Clayton was going to attack him. She can't be trying to help him. She led him to this torture.

"How do you know?"

"Look at him Clayton! He looks broken. He looks nothing like the big bad strong Warrior Weapon anymore. I don't think he ever wanted to. If he had, why wouldn't he answer you? Why would he sit and look at the floor if he doesn't feel horrible about killing people?"

"He can be a good liar, Victoria."

"Clayton, I thought you were better than that." A single tear streams down Victoria's face.

Aaron sits there and listens to them. Victoria was right. He does feel horrible. At the same time, Clayton is right. Aaron could easily be lying to them. After all, how can anyone trust a killer?

"Should we allow him to stay here? What if this is just a ploy to kill us all, right under our noses?"

"Clayton Whitmore!"

"No." Aaron speaks for the first time since.

"What is that?" Clayton sounds surprised that Aaron

even spoke words.

"Simon made me."

"Why?" Clayton and Victoria ask the question at the exact same moment, but with two different tones.

"I don't know." Aaron wishes he could speak. He is going to seem unwilling to answer. He hates himself.

"Did you want to?" Victoria stands behind Aaron's chair and places her hands on his shoulders. If he were in Revelation, he would have jumped. Why does he feel safe with her touching him?

"I don't know."

"How do you not know!" Clayton slams his hands on top of Victoria's. She slaps them off. Aaron can't see what kind of looks the two are giving each other.

"Clayton, give him a chance to talk! Aaron, why did you do it?"

"Jonathan." This is the only way Aaron can justify doing what he did. His brother, his only family, the reason Aaron can ever dream of happiness.

"Who's Jonathan?" Victoria moves from behind Aaron to in front of him. She pushes Clayton over, and squats in front of Aaron. She puts her hand on his forearm, right on his scar. It feels cool against his skin. Why did his body become warm? Normally he is cold to the touch.

"Brother."

"Aaron, can I ask you something?" Victoria's words are calm and filled with concern and curiosity.

"Yes." Aaron doesn't want to deny any questions. He is

already in trouble.

"Are you holding anything back?"

"No." Aaron is stupid, but not stupid enough to hold information from the people who kept him alive.

"Do you want to destroy us?" Clayton interrupts Victoria, who had just opened her mouth to speak. She turns her head and sends him a dirty look.

"No. Simon." Aaron answers Clayton truthfully. He only wants to destroy Simon. He wants Simon to suffer.

"Aaron, can you describe how you came here?" Clayton's demeanor shows that he could care less about how Aaron arrived. Victoria is asking easy questions for Aaron to answer. Does she know he can't talk?

"Woods."

Victoria stands up. In her face Aaron can see grief and sadness. She looks over at Clayton. Aaron watches her every move. He feels the corners of his mouth turn down a little. Clayton looks confused as he listens to what Victoria has to say.

"Clayton, it's not that he doesn't want to talk to us. He can't."

11 Language

Trees sway as the gusts blow by Aaron, throwing a cool sensation over his exposed skin. Occasionally, a small shiver runs through his spine. He would prefer the warmth inside the compound, but he needs to clear his head. Everything he heard, all of the new information, the new emotions, the pain, he needs to run away from it all.

The roof has always been his best friend. He just lies for hours, not moving or speaking, just enjoying the view of the sky. Normally he would prefer the storm, but the calm has become his favorite. There hasn't been a storm since he came. He wonders why. Storms used to occur at least once a month. There hasn't been one in four or five months. There could have been one when he was out cold.

His jacket is providing some barrier to the cold, but he wishes he had changed. He changed right after meeting with

Clayton into a graphic t-shirt and jeans with holes in them. He regrets not putting on something warmer. He knew he was coming to the roof. His stupidity amazes him sometimes. He rubs his hands on his upper arm. There is a slight ache, but he feels little pain. There are new scars everywhere, but no outsider would have guessed he was viciously attacked a few weeks ago.

Someone comes on the roof. Aaron's entire body tenses, but he doesn't move. He doesn't want to know who it is. If it's a Soldier, he might finish the job. If it's Victoria, he just isn't in the mood to talk to anyone or even try to listen. He doubts it is Clayton. Aaron has never seen Clayton unless he is called to him.

Wordlessly, the person slowly sits next to Aaron. It can't be a Soldier. Soldiers don't have long hair.

"Hey," Victoria simply says after a long stretch of silence. Aaron makes a noise, not quite a grunt, but not a word, to acknowledge her greeting.

After another few moments of silence, she turns to her right to look at Aaron. He isn't sure if he should ignore her or sit up.

"We should talk. Or I can talk and you can listen. Either way, I'm not waiting for an answer. I don't hate you, Aaron. I'm not mad either. I was shocked to learn that you are Revelation's Warrior Weapon. But that's where I messed up. You were their weapon, but now you aren't. I wish I could talk where you can understand me. I just don't know how."

Aaron can barely understand her, but he knows she

feels bad. He wants to tell her that she shouldn't feel bad about anything. He deserves it all. He looks to his left, intending to look at her face, but then he notices a pen. It's stuffed in her pocket, almost as if it is waiting for Aaron to grab it.

He sits up and quickly takes the pen. Victoria is shocked at the sudden movement. Now that the cat is out of the bag, Aaron feels no need to hide his speed anymore. He takes the cap off, but instead of sticking it on the back end of the pen, he holds it between his teeth. He has always done this, and doesn't know why. He never even notices that quirk anymore. But Victoria does.

"Well that's one way to keep track of the cap." He can't think of a response. Instead of trying, he uses his hand as a broom and brushes away any rocks or dirt that may be on the floor of the roof. Then, he leans over and writes. Victoria can't see what he is doing. He intended to show her, but he blocks her view with his body.

I can't talk because I don't know how to form words or sentences. I can write and read.

Aaron sits up and looks at Victoria. Disappointed, Aaron puts the cap back on the pen. She must not care that he can communicate.

"What's that look for? And what are you doing?" Aaron realizes she just can't see what he is doing. He is too stupid to be living. Of course, bending over would block her view. He wishes his brain was as efficient as his eyes.

"Look." Aaron points to his feet. He feels like a fool. Why would she have any reason to care that Aaron can write? She looks, at first not wanting to, but then her facial expression changes. She grabs the pen from Aaron's hand and smiles.

Maybe one day I can teach you to speak.

She gives Aaron her pen and then walks away. He waits for her to leave before he lies down again. He tries not to think of anything. He just lies on the roof for hours, avoiding the fact he will eventually need to react to what Victoria wrote with the pen. He doesn't want to get too excited. Maybe she doesn't mean it.. For now, he just drifts off into a light sleep, hoping to wake tomorrow morning peacefully.

As Aaron sleeps, the night sky stays the same, no clouds, shooting stars, or anything interesting. The forest around the compound is quiet. Some would think too quiet, but there is nothing abnormal about the forest not having activity. After all, hardly any animals exist on the planet anymore.

When morning comes, dawn's light creeps over Aaron's face and he awakes peacefully, like he had hoped for. He could have gone inside and slept, but why? He can think of no logical reason for sleeping inside or out. Last night, he needed a break.

He looks down at his feet and reads the messages again. Permanently etched into the concrete is Aaron's chance for knowledge. If he allows her teach him, he can ask questions and learn more things. Books have little to no value. Nearly everything mentioned is gone. The history of the past world has never been recorded, at least not that Aaron knows of. Why would anyone publish it? Most everyone knows it. Speaking to living people is the only way Aaron can learn more.

He wants to sit down with Clayton and ask him millions of questions. He wants to know more about this God and who He is. He wants to know more about the past. Who is Clayton's father? What was he like? Why did he start Reformation? Why does everyone else hate Revelation? Aaron knows why he does, but what about all the other reasons?

Aaron stands up. He could walk to the latch and go down the ladder. Instead, he sprints to the edge of the roof and jumps. He grabs onto a tree branch and dangles in mid air. He decides to climb the tree. He quickly looks for all the sturdy branches and starts to jump from one to the other, not caring who sees or what sounds he makes. The trees rustle, but he is enjoying himself. Once he reaches the top, he sits on the sturdiest branch he can.

Should he go down? He knows he should. But he doesn't want to. He plans to dodge Victoria and Clayton. He wants to avoid being depressed with facts about his killings or about the past.

After a few short moments of debate, he reluctantly jumps from the top of the tree to the very bottom. The impact would break most people, but he walks away with no problem. The freedom feels good, to show who he really is.

"Aaron!" A female voice calls for him, sounding almost frantic. He looks to the left for the source of the voice, but finds no one. It sounds like Victoria, and it would make sense. Are there any other girls in the compound, or is she the only one?

"Aaron!" This time a male voice calls, just as frantic as the girl's. It comes from the right, unlike the girl's. Aaron can't pinpoint where the voice is coming from. He didn't hear it as clearly as he should have. Whoever is calling is probably walking towards the north, shouting the way he is walking instead of calling to the south where Aaron is. The girl seems to be walking towards him.

Within seconds of leaving his position, he nearly runs Victoria over. He sprinted too quickly. He should watch his speed. He can't run anyone over or hurt anyone. He needs to watch where he is
going and who is around when he is running.

"There you are. Clayton! I found him!" Victoria is breathing heavily. Sweat is slowly falling from her forehead to her chin. Worry takes over every feature of her person, but slowly relief takes over. Why is she worried? What exactly is she worried about? "Please don't do that again!"

"What?" Aaron isn't sure what he did that she doesn't like.

"You were just gone! Not in your room, your bed, the roof, the cafeteria, the bathroom, the cellar, anywhere! Where were you?" Victoria is nearly out of breath.

"I'd love to know." Aaron turns his head to the right, finding Clayton. How has he yet to completely recognize Clayton? He knew who it was when he was attacked by the Soldiers. How can he not recognize Clayton after that?

Aaron chooses not to respond and simply looks and gestures to the top of the trees with his head. To further prove his point before the two ask any more questions, he takes off running and within thirty seconds sits on the top of a great Redwood.

"Come on down." Clayton shouts to Aaron. Not that he wants to, but he listens. He needs to be good and listen. Clayton is the reason he isn't dead. He should be grateful, and he is.

Aaron jumps down instead of climbing. Why should he when jumping takes less effort? He lands just inches from Victoria. She squeaks and jumps back, grabbing her chest with one hand and covering her mouth with the other. Clayton looks between Aaron and Victoria, and then begins to laugh uncontrollably.

"Why does that scare you?" Clayton asks between laughs. Victoria blushes at her embarrassment, but then sends an evil glare to Clayton.

"I wasn't scared. I was surprised." Victoria tries to defend herself.

"Uh huh, sure Victoria." Clayton continues to laugh at Victoria.

Aaron isn't sure of what he should do while the two bicker.

Both Clayton and Victoria are so similar. The two would never admit it, but Aaron can tell there is a bond. He thinks about Revelation. After a few months at Reformation, he has noticed almost everyone is the same color and build, and there isn't really much of an age difference. Revelation is different. Almost every puppet is different. Other than Aaron and his brother, there are no relatives or anyone that look remotely similar. There are no bonds between the puppets. All different races, ages, heights, weights, skill levels are welcomed and utilized at Revelation. Every puppet has something new and different.

The two continue to bicker, but Aaron stops paying attention. He is looking for something to write with and finds a thin metal bar on the ground. It is all he needs to communicate with Victoria and Clayton.

"Anyway, sorry about that Aaron. She can be such a child sometimes, don't you agree? Only Victoria can be scared by someone landing next to her." Clayton is still laughing lightly.

"Clayton! Oh hey, what are you writing?" Victoria walks closer to Aaron.

Aaron steps away from where he is writing, showing them information they should know.

There are no two puppets alike at Revelation. Everyone has a different skill or talent that Simon uses. You need the same thing here. Everyone here is very similar. You all have bonds. They may be the reason you die. In Revelation, it's every man or woman for themselves.

"You can write?" Clayton grabs Aaron by his shoulders and looks Aaron straight in the eye. Aaron can't tell if he is angry or surprised. He simply nods his head.

"I was going to tell you that he showed me he can write last night, but then we couldn't find him. Clayton, I think we can teach him to talk and understand speech. He seems really smart. We should start now." Victoria smiles and looks at Aaron.

Victoria walks over to Clayton and Aaron. She knocks Clayton's hands off Aaron. She doesn't say a word to Aaron, but simply makes a gesture for him to give her the stick. He gives it to her, and then she squats down and writes.

Do you want to learn to speak?

"He should learn to fight to. I don't want a repeat of the attack." Clayton is speaking directly to Victoria.

And fight to protect yourself?

She looks up at him. Aaron nods his head. He doesn't need a stick to answer that question. Both are privileges he has never been allowed to have in his life.

The three walk back towards the compound. There is no one outside, but activity can be heard inside. When they enter, all activity ceases. Previously happy faces turn to scornful, angry looks. Aaron looks down, unable to meet the eyes of anyone in the compound.

"Make one wrong look at Aaron, and I will personally give you your punishment. Continue your work." Clayton's voice rings through the halls. His word is law. No one other than Victoria has challenged it as far as Aaron knows. Even Victoria is careful when she does challenge Clayton.

Through the winding halls they walk until they reach their destination. Aaron has no idea where they are going, but

Clayton and Victoria do. Once again, they stop abruptly and open the door quickly. Aaron hopes one day he can do the same.

The trio enters a smaller, more private gym. It's a smaller version of the gym where the Soldiers train, except there is no room to run around. There are no windows, just flickering florescent lights. Other than the door they came through, only one directly in front of them exists.

"No one comes in here but us three. That door in front of you leads to where you are staying, which has connections to both my room and Clayton's. We are planning on teaching you to fight, but when we have free time we will teach you to speak. I'll write this down so you can understand." Victoria's excitement radiates as she goes through the other door to grab paper for Aaron. He understands a little of what she said, but not much.

"I want you to rest for another week. I'm going to leave Victoria to teach you to start speaking. Good luck, Aaron. I'll see you in a week to teach you to fight."

Victoria comes back into the room just as Clayton takes his leave through the rear door. She doesn't look at all surprised by his exit.

Are you ready, Aaron?

Yes.

Aaron.

"Aaron." Victoria says his name. He looks up at her, waiting
for her to say more. She points to the paper and begins writing. Aaron directs his attention to what she writes.

I will write a word, and then say it. Then you try to say it, okay?

"Aaron." Aaron has never read his name and been able to say it. He has never been able to say anything he can write, for the most part.

Victoria looks Aaron directly in the eye, something no one has ever done before today, and smiles. Both she and Clayton have so much trust in him not to turn on them and kill them.

Victoria.

"Victoria." Aaron and Victoria say the word at the exact same time.

Weapon.

"Weapon." Victoria says the word, but Aaron can't repeat it as easily. He can say weapon all day long, but reading it aloud is making it hard. He wants to learn.

For the next week, all Aaron does is repeat what Victoria says. Soon, he picks up on how certain words and phrases are supposed to sound. At some point during the week, he doesn't need her to read the whole sentence out loud, only parts he has no idea how to say. After just a week, he learns how speak basically. He understands most of what he is saying.

"Morning, Clayton." Aaron immediately greets Clayton as soon as he walks through the door. Aaron is sitting in a chair facing the door. He has been waiting for the week to pass.

"Um, morning. How did the lessons go?" Clayton looks at Aaron strangely. No one should learn how to speak as quickly as Aaron has. Then again, no one should be able to do anything Aaron does.

"Good. I still write better, but I can talk more." Aaron stands up. He is fully healed from all the wounds he received from the Soldiers. He is glad he can speak, but he wants to learn to fight. He needs to in order to kill Simon more painfully.

"Duck." Aaron isn't understanding Clayton is saying. Why is Clayton talking about a bird?

A knife flies by his head, scratching his ear. Before Aaron can process what happened, Clayton throws another knife, aiming for Aaron's throat. Aaron moves to the side, but he is still grazed by the knife on his throat.

"Duck means get lower to the ground to avoid being hit by a weapon. Understand?" Clayton walks directly in front of Aaron.

"Yes sir."

Aaron tries to take a step back. He doesn't know what Clayton is going to do next. As he tries, Clayton punches Aaron on his right cheek, and then his left. The force causes Aaron to lose his footing and he falls. Clayton kicks him hard in the ribs. Aaron groans.

"Always expect the unexpected, Aaron." Clayton offers Aaron his hand to help him up. Aaron takes his hand. Just as Clayton begins to lift Aaron, he punches him again.

Aaron falls to the floor again. He glares at Clayton. He tries his hardest not to rely on his eyes. Instead, he charges Clayton. Clayton lifts both of his arms near his face with his hands balled in fists.

As Aaron comes within a foot of Clayton, Clayton goes to punch Aaron, but punches air. Aaron is behind Clayton and punches him as hard as he can in the back of the head.

Clayton falls to the floor. He rolls over and looks at Aaron.

"You just might have what it takes to kill Simon. You might make it out alive."

12 Information

Four months have passed since Aaron first woke from the attack. Once again, he finds himself on the roof. He isn't sitting or lying like normal. He is walking around in circles and squares.

"Hey you! It's dinner!" Victoria's voice rings clearly from the hatch leading to the hallway below. Aaron looks out to the horizon. The sun is low to the ground, signaling the end to the day.

He walks over and jumps down the opening. The newest members of the compound freeze in fear. They aren't sure what he is. The Soldiers still hold their grudge, but they are used to him by now. Aaron no longer feels the need to look down in shame. In the past, he would have stayed normal and done nothing out of the ordinary. He would have never met anyone's eyes. He knows he is a changed person. He simply nods their way and then looks at Victoria.

"What's on the menu?" Aaron is hoping for something slightly edible.

"I'm not sure. We aren't eating with the Soldiers. Clayton wants to have a private meeting."

"When does he ever not meet with us in private?" Aaron bumps Victoria's shoulder with his own before smiling at his own sarcasm. Would he have ever had the courage to do this four months ago? Never. Victoria chuckles before leading the way.

"You know, neither you or Clayton ever taught me the secret to this labyrinth." Aaron makes the statement randomly. He has been at Reformation for almost a year and still isn't sure how to find his way around.

"There isn't one." Victoria doesn't elaborate on her answer.

"Sure there isn't." Aaron wonders if she is telling the truth.

"Honestly, I can't tell you what half these doors lead to. Some are rooms, others are storage, and some I truly don't know. I just memorized the way to rooms I do know. I don't even think Clayton knows them all."

"How can he not?" Clayton is the leader. Leaders have to know everything. How can a leader not know all the rooms?

"Well, his dad is the one who built this compound. His dad designed all the quirky aspects, not Clayton. His dad trained him until the day he died, but Clayton only shadowed his dad. I doubt his dad went into every single room."

"Actually my dad did." Clayton stands in the doorway. "Ready for dinner you two?"

"Sure are. Hopefully it's better than what they serve in the cafeteria." Aaron no longer has a filter on his mouth. Four months of learning, four months of bruises and laughter, four months of speech lessons have created a new person.

Aaron previously would have never said a word, stayed far from people, watched what he said in order to avoid a beating. He would have never been able to communicate with people. Now he jokes with Simon's enemy. Jonathan would love to see Aaron like this. One day Aaron is going back for Jonathan. He needs to become stronger and smarter so he can take out Simon at the same time.

"I would hope so. I did go out and hunt it down myself." Clayton ushers the two inside the room and closes the door.

"What did you catch this time?" Victoria asks out of curiosity.

"A doe. It reminded me of you, Victoria. But it put up much more of a fight."

"Why do you always insult me?"

"Can we eat before you two kill each other? I'm hungry and would like to enjoy my meal not covered in blood." Aaron wonders how they always have something to tease each other with.

"You two sit down. I'm going to put on some music." Clayton walks off, heading behind a few book cases to the far east side of the room. Aaron looks at Victoria, giving her his best confused look.

"It's something to listen to." Victoria tells Aaron before he asks his question.

"Like?"

"I'm not sure how to explain it. In a minute you'll hear it for yourself." Moments later a slow melody comes from Aaron's right.

"I can't find anything more interesting. Classical piano okay?" Clayton sits down at the table.

"Better than that God awful Michael Jackson and Elvis music," Victoria groans.

"How dare you insult the kings?" Clayton slams his hands on the table.

"Who? And what is a piano?" Aaron never would have asked questions in the past, but now he has no problem with it.

"A piano is a musical instrument that plays a range of different sounds. Those horrible singers are some of Clayton's favorites." Victoria explains everything to Aaron. She has patience with him and answers every question he asks.

"They are the best musicians on the planet!" Clayton slams his hands on the table. "I wish I had been alive a century and a half before now so I could have seen them. It must have been a wonderful experience for those who were alive."

"That was a long time ago." Twenty years has felt like forever to Aaron. He can't imagine how long a hundred and fifty years would feel.

"Well, Aaron, the world only ended around eighty years

ago. It hasn't been that long since the New World, this world, started its fight for survival." Victoria cuts her meat into small pieces as she talks.

"Eat both of you. But thank you for bringing up the end, Victoria. That's why I wanted to talk to you both. I think now is the time." Clayton takes a large bite of the deer before continuing, not bothering to close his mouth or swallow. "We need to start planning to take out Revelation. Aaron, what do you know about Revelation?"

"Uh." Aaron moves the piece of meat he just cut around his plate. He knows a lot, but he isn't sure how well he can explain it all. It would probably take more than one dinner to tell it all. "It's a lot to tell."

"Aaron, if you haven't noticed, Clayton and I don't do much all day. You have given us so much more to do." Victoria talks calmly and takes a sip of water before putting the meat in her mouth.

"Normally we only plan for those who are going to die. Aaron, with you, we can plan a victory. We have plenty of time. Just tell us everything." Clayton eats more of his food.

Aaron takes a few moments before he begins to speak.

"Well, I don't know where to start. One thing you should know is there are mutations and experiments at Revelation. Simon is sick and twisted. I was his first human subject and his second experiment. Before me, there were a lot of Gelchorks. I don't know if they are wolves or dogs, but they are a canine of some sort. I know the most about them because I relate to them. We both have heightened senses and we were both created the same way."

"So they are a pack of dogs? Is there a reason you are mentioning them?" Victoria begins the questioning. Aaron isn't sure if this dinner is going to be an interrogation, but it already feels like it.

"Gelchorks aren't creatures that you should ignore." Aaron replies. "They stand eight feet tall with bones sticking from their spine. Once their flesh is torn it stays torn unless another Gelchork rips it off for food. They have one head, until you make them mad or injure them in battle. They can split their head into two, revealing three rows of crooked, rotting pointed teeth that can rip though almost anything. Don't underestimate a Gelchork."

"You said you and Gelchorks were made the same way. Do you know how?" Clayton leans forward.

"No. I just know it was in the basement. It was dark and I was injected with this blue liquid into my eye." Aaron looks down. "I don't really remember much else. The only thing that stands out is the blue liquid also has this orange thing in it. Sorry, I don't really remember much of the details."

"If you didn't tell us another thing tonight, we would still leave with more than we had. Don't be sorry. No one ever told you to remember it all," Victoria reassures Aaron.

Before continuing, Aaron picks at his plate a little more. His food is starting to become cold. Both Clayton and Victoria already have finished.

"The compound is concealed really well. It has a long stretch of land on all four sides before the wall that protects it can be seen." Aaron takes another bite before continuing. "There are two buildings, the compound and the training area. The training area is a small building with only one floor. The compound is small. It is two floors high, but houses all of the puppets. Simon only keeps the best in this compound." Aaron takes a drink of water. He dislikes talking for extended periods of time. "Wherever there is a compound, he has one or two within two hundred or so miles. This is the only exception. Because he keeps his best puppets there, he only has one. Compared to the travel time of the other compounds, it is really close. It only took me two months to slowly walk here."

"Really? So, if you ran, would it only take you a month?" Victoria leans closer towards Aaron.

"Probably. If I were sprinting, I could get there in a day." Aaron isn't sure how long it would take.

"Do you know why you were created?" Clayton asks him yet another difficult question.

After that question, Aaron stops noting who asks what. He knows none of the questions are meant to be offensive. He refuses to allow the questions to bother him.

Several hours pass before anyone even notices that they are starting to become tired. Clayton and Victoria are glued to Aaron, soaking in every word. So many important details pass through his lips, informing Clayton and Victoria of everything they here missed.

"Wait, so can you explain—" Victoria tries to ask her question, but is cut off mid-sentence.

"Victoria, I'm sure he's tired of talking." Clayton

interrupts Victoria. "Why don't we all just continue this in the morning?"

"That would be nice." Aaron is exhausted. Victoria and Clayton asked so many questions. He is tired of explaining everything.

"Alright." Victoria's voice sounds disappointed, but it doesn't show on her face.

"Good night you two. Victoria, don't keep him up much longer. You need your rest so you don't look like a sea witch tomorrow." Clayton takes off running towards the other end of the room, slamming a door before Victoria registers his insult.

Victoria stands still. She begins to take a step, but then she decides not to move. She sighs and turns to Aaron. He is standing with his arms crossed, staring at her.

"I want to sleep." Aaron has no idea how to walk to his room from here. He is tired.

"First we are going to talk." Victoria crosses her arms and looks at him.

"I've done that all night." Aaron doesn't want to talk anymore. He knows he won't win against her. She will find some way to keep him up longer.

"Just follow me." Victoria starts to walk away.

Whether Aaron wants to or not, he needs to follow Victoria. She is his only chance of going back to his room to sleep. It has to be at least midnight by now.

She walks quickly and almost mindlessly, as if she has taken this path every single day of her life and has no need to pay attention to where she is going. She turns to her left and

Revelation

mechanically opens a door and then steps in. Aaron follows.

"Close the door," says Victoria. "This is my room in case you are wondering."

"Actually I was. But you're lying." Aaron replies.

"What?" She turns around and looks at him. Her eyes are wider than normal.

"You are very proper with your sentences when you are lying. I'm guessing this was Daryl's room." Victoria looks down.

"Yeah, it was. It is my room now."

"Why are we here?" Aaron can't understand what she is trying to do.

"You should have met him. It's scary how much you two are alike." She pauses and turns from Aaron. He can see her move her hands to her face, most likely wiping away tears. He looks down to the floor. The past is depressing, especially when it affects those he is close to now. "Do you know why Clayton and I are good friends?"

"Are you guys related?" Aaron isn't sure of Clayton and Victoria's relationship.

"No. We are far from it. I have only known him for five years. His dad created the test you took. He wanted the perfect army, so he used the test to find everyone's advantages. It's nearly impossible to achieve the same score on both tests, but Clayton and I did. We are the only two so far. Because of that, we are kept on the sidelines as trainers for both the Brains and the Soldiers. We have both lost someone special to this war, my Daryl and his dad." Victoria sits down on the bed. Aaron stays standing near the door.

"He must have been special."

"He was. We had been told by our parents we were to marry in five years when we were ten. I didn't like the idea. He was my best friend. I didn't want to marry him. I grew to love him as more than a friend. We ran away when we were fourteen. We had heard about the war and wanted to destroy Revelation. Boy, were we stupid. You know, every night he always brought me a flower. It was actually a weed, but he didn't know." A tear slides down Victoria's face.

"I'm sorry." Aaron has nothing else to say. He is the reason Daryl isn't here. What is he supposed to say at a time like this?

"I can forgive you. You are a different person. You didn't have a choice under Simon. Now you do."

There is a silence that fills the room. Aaron takes a seat in the only chair in the room while Victoria continues to sit on her bed.

"Aaron, what do you know about yourself?"

"Not much. My parents are dead and I grew up in Revelation. My last name is Stoppa and I'm nineteen and I have a brother, Jonathan." Aaron recites what he knows. He doesn't know much else about himself.

"Huh. Do you think Jonathan knows more about you two?" Victoria's curiosity is beginning to show again.

"Yes." Jonathan knows much more. He was older when Simon entered their lives. Jonathan has to remember more.

Silence takes over the room again. Aaron isn't sure how much time passes. He doesn't count the time like normal. He avoids moving or thinking. He enjoys the silence.

"Why don't you just stay in here tonight? I'm too lazy to walk you back." Victoria breaks the silence.

"Where am I going to sleep?"

"In my bed. Where else?" Victoria doesn't wait for Aaron to protest. She climbs in and begins to doze off. She must have forgotten to change clothes. "Don't forget to turn off the light."

Aaron stares at her for a moment, but then he goes and shuts

the light off. He doesn't need much light to see. He isn't sure he should stay in the same bed as her. It feels wrong. He has never slept with another person. It seems as if it would be awkward. But after months of comfort, he doesn't want to sleep in a chair or on the floor.

He slowly walks to the right side of the bed. She is curled up on her left side, breathing slowly and softly. Her room is hot and has no window for him to open. He knows he will wake at least ten times if he falls asleep. Awkwardly, he strips off his shirt and lies down. He moves slowly, hoping not to wake her.

Victoria is already deeply asleep. Aaron knows she must be exhausted. He lies as close as he can to the edge. He feels stiff and awkward at first, but the sound of her breathing is almost soothing, and soon he finds himself drifting off to sleep.

He wakes hours later to a light being turned on suddenly. He grabs the sheet on his chest and pulls it over his eyes.

"Why?" Aaron groans. Why is she up so early?

Victoria screams bloody murder. Aaron jump out of the bed and in a blink of an eye he is grabbing her shoulders, looking at her, trying to find out what is wrong without saying anything.

"I forgot you stayed in here," she says to him, still shaking.

"How did you forget? You basically made me stay in here last night." He releases Victoria and sits down.

He isn't used to being woken from a deep sleep. Why did he sleep so well? He isn't sure. He rubs his hands on his eyes and yawns.

He turns to look at Victoria. He starts to ask her if she will walk him back to his room, but stops. She is staring at him.

"What?" Aaron asks her, trying to figure out why she isn't doing anything but staring.

"Aaron, how many of those scars are from battle?"

The question throws him off guard. He isn't expecting that. He wonders how she knows he has a body full of scars, but then he notices his shirt on the floor. He is sweating a lot. He remembers he took off his shirt to go to sleep.

"Less than you think." Aaron tries to speak quietly.

She is still staring at him. He tries to ignore her. He grabs his shirt off the floor. He decides not to put it on because he is going to take a shower once he leaves. He walks to the door, but Victoria stands in front of it. She won't allow him leave.

"What do you mean?" Victoria crosses her arms.

"Exactly what I said. Now move." Aaron tries to go around her, but it doesn't work.

"No. Where are they from?"

"Simon." Aaron doesn't want to talk about it. He has no idea why he answered her. He looks down at the floor.

Revelation

"How? There are so many. None of them look like they were taken care of." Victoria looks at him, but Aaron refuses to look at her.

"Tending to a wound is for the weak, Aaron. If you can't survive, then you don't deserve to be alive." Aaron's voice is dead, emotionless. He is quoting Simon. The feelings of all the experiments and tortures are coming back full force.

"What did he do to you?" Victoria goes to touch Aaron. He slaps her hands away. He tries to leave again. She still won't allow him. He groans, turns around, and walks over to her bed and sits down. He covers his face with his hand.

"Experiments." Aaron mumbles. He wants to finish this conversation quickly. "After my eyes, there weren't many more. Occasionally he would inject more of whatever he used originally to see if there was improvement in my eyes. There never was. If there wasn't, I was punished for not being able to improve. Those punishments were the worst. Just three months before I left to come here, he tried again." Aaron sighs. He hates talking about Simon. The more he talks, the more he wants to kill him. "It's the newest scar on my back. You can find it easily. He splattered acid on me. As it stopped tearing away at my flesh, he would add more. It lasted for three hours. My shoulder blade was exposed by that point. Then he took a dagger to it and pounded at it until it shattered."

Victoria looks at Aaron. He can't see her horrified expression.

"Then there were the endurance tests." Aaron isn't sure why he is continuing. "He called them training. I was lit on fire, forced to fight Gelchorks, stabbed, injected with various poisons, starved, skinned, forced to endure whatever his puppets wanted to do. Normally, after they beat me, I couldn't move."

Aaron stands up and walks to the door. He puts his hand on the door knob. He hates talking about Simon. He hates when people ask questions. He wants to kill Simon. He wants him dead.

Aaron punches the door with his left hand over and over again. Victoria watches and does nothing.

"If I didn't endure pain, then I was torn apart mentally with descriptions of images, statistics, anything to cause me to mentally break. Each time was worse and worse."

Three tears slowly travel down his face. He hates talking about the past. Victoria hasn't said a word. She comes up behind Aaron and puts her hand on his right shoulder, the one with the nastiest scar.

"Do you want him dead?"

"Yes."

"We need to go find Clayton."

13   Plan of Attack

Two months filled with restless nights and little sleep pass. Over one thousand hours of planning have passed, and they are almost near perfection. Clayton, Aaron, and Victoria have been planning how to destroy Revelation. After Aaron's description, Victoria and Clayton are determined Revelation needs to be wiped off the face of the planet.

"Go over the plan again." Victoria is bursting with energy, proud of the three of them for coming so far in such a small amount of time.

"We will take the army to the north end, farthest from the Gelchorks." Clayton says to Aaron. "They aren't alerted by much during the day time. If we go at high noon, they won't be a problem. We will have to wait it out, but if we go during a storm, we won't be detected."

"That won't work. During a storm, no one is looking for

invaders, but the Gelchorks are on high alert. There is too much stimuli for them to rest. You need to go in the opposite direction of the wind. If it's blowing to the east, come from the east. Unless it's near the Gelchorks, that is your best bet." Aaron knows a storm can be both an advantage and disadvantage.

"Are you sure? Won't the snipers be on alert?" Victoria asks quickly before Clayton says anything else.

"They never have been." Aaron tries to reassure Victoria. "Even if they are, I'm sure you can manage. They aren't going to be able to see through the rain, unless you are sitting right in front of the window. Then, yeah, they will see you."

"Aaron, if we do tip off the Gelchorks, what do we do?" Victoria asks out of curiosity.

"Kill the Alpha." Aaron nonchalantly answers Victoria's question. It is the only obvious answer.

"Are you crazy?" Clayton raises his eyebrow at Aaron after Victoria's question.

"No. Okay, imagine this scenario, Victoria. If someone came in and killed Clayton and me quickly, wouldn't you listen to them, just to save yourself?" Aaron looks her straight in the eye as he talks.

"Yeah." Victoria says after thinking for a few moments.

"Same with the Gelchorks. Simon kills a few when he needs their loyalty. They breed like rabbits. Killing a few doesn't matter. What does matter is having them know who to listen to. They don't howl at an enemy. They only howl when they want something to kill. If you behead the Alpha, the Beta will make sure all the others know who the new Alpha is." Aaron doesn't take his eyes off Victoria.

"Are you positive?" Victoria redirects her eyes so she isn't looking into Aaron's.

"I'm pretty sure." Aaron wonders how Victoria can think he isn't sure. He lived there for fifteen years. He knows almost everything about the Gelchorks.

"We will enter opposite of the wind. Then we will go to the west side of the building, which conveniently has no windows. We will enter into the basement through the outside basement. The other half will take out the training room. We will have to make sure it is a day Simon refuses to leave his room." Clayton repeats the plan to Aaron, making sure he knows the plan inside and out.

"He won't leave. He hates storms. Unless he is already outside, he will stay inside. When Simon is inside, most everyone wants to be as far away as possible." Aaron knows Simon's habits too well.

"Then that shouldn't be a problem." Victoria is pleased with the plan so far, as are Clayton and Aaron.

"Okay, Victoria, Simon isn't your problem so you are taking out the training room, right?" Clayton asks. He is trying to make sure the entire plan goes smoothly.

"Yeah." Victoria begins to repeat her part of the plan perfectly. "While you and Aaron go into the compound, I will take the most people with quick reflexes since we are probably going to have more enemies. Luckily, we will have more men than them. If we take them all out, we will make sure to force the Gelchorks on our side, and then go aid everyone."

"Aaron, what are you doing?" Clayton asks, curious for details.

"I'm going in first. I'll freeze up as many as I can, and then I'm heading for Simon."

"Are you sure you want to take him on your own?" Victoria looks at Aaron.

"I used to be afraid. I'm not anymore. I can take him. Victoria, just make sure you don't kill my brother. He looks like me, but a little older and with shorter hair."

"I'll make sure Victoria doesn't take him out. I'm sure he would love to stay with you." Clayton pauses. "I feel like this is too simple of a plan."

"Clayton, I'm sure Aaron won't lead us to death." Victoria speaks reassuringly.

"Just don't forget, these are the best of everyone. Just because they have fewer men means nothing. They all have their best skills ready to go at any time." Aaron's worst fear is Reformation losing everyone in this battle. He hopes that doesn't happen.

"You have to believe in us Aaron. My father trained me for eight years before I took this job over, and I'm still here." Clayton says softly to Aaron.

"Five years later, I still haven't forgotten who I'm up against." Victoria smiles.

"Just be careful." Aaron couldn't bear to lose anyone to Simon.

"The same goes for you." Clayton and Victoria look at each other, realizing they have been good friends for far too long if they can say the same thing in the same tone at the exact same time.

"We should go eat. I'm starving." Aaron talks without thinking now. He knows what starving means. He has been there before. Now he talks just like everyone else, changing the meaning. He can't believe how far he has come.

The three stand, ready to go to Clayton's own small kitchen and grab something decent to eat. They have already discussed how they will hold a compound wide meeting soon. Just as they exit the room, an old Soldier in tattered clothing greets them.

"Clayton, Simon has sent a message to all the compounds."

"What?" Victoria can't contain her shock. Clayton lacks any emotion on his face. Aaron feels his heart drop. This means Simon knows where he is.

"Recite it word for word."

"Aaron, I know you are hiding at one of the Reformation compounds. If you thought your actions had no consequences, you are a fool, stupider than I thought. Since the day you ran, I have been slowly and painfully torturing Jonathan. It has been exactly one year since you ran. If you don't return very soon, I will kill Jonathan, and then I will kill you."

14   Tortured

After only hours of scrambling, the entire compound is sitting in the basement. Word spread rapidly throughout the compound. A threat from Revelation is big news in Reformation. Even the Soldiers who despise Aaron are sitting in the basement. Everyone here wants Revelation gone.

Only a few people are missing. The bravest of everyone are outside, watching out for any enemies. Aaron wonders if Daryl would be there if he hadn't killed him. Those who are outside are the only hope Clayton, Aaron, and Victoria have for keeping everyone safe. If any of those who are guarding see an enemy, he will lock down the entire compound, which will shut down everything and lock everyone inside the basement. Aaron hopes nothing like that will happen. Hopefully Simon will give him time to receive the message and make a decision.

"Stupid." From under his breath, the word can barely be

Revelation

heard. Even though everyone has been rushing to organize the meeting for hours, it has felt like minutes for Aaron. He hasn't moved from the floor. In a lonely corner of the basement, near the Zentarium filters, Aaron sits, curled in a small ball, refusing to look at anyone. Muttering is the only sign that Aaron is alive.

"We are going to begin." Clayton's voice rings throughout the basement and everyone shuts their mouth and looks at him. Normally Aaron would be in awe at his ability to balance normal and control, but tonight he just wants to go drive a tree through Simon's throat. "This is an emergency meeting, the first one since our creation fourteen years ago. Simon has sent a threat to one of our own. I don't care if you don't personally like him. He is one of us now. I forgot all I heard about every single one of you, and I have done the same for Aaron."

There is a small murmuring in the crowd, but a low growl from Clayton silences everyone. Victoria is standing by his side, but she isn't paying attention. Instead, she is looking at Aaron.

"Aaron knows more about Revelation than anyone in this room. He knows the leader, Simon, and he knows all of the members he hires. He has even informed us of the fact only the best of the worst personalities from around the world are allowed to enter the compound. We have formulated a plan. It's rather —"

"Aaron." Victoria interrupts Clayton. "You need to present this. Without you, neither Clayton nor I can ever have anything to share. This is a three part plan, and only you know what you are doing the best, not us." Everyone looks at her, including Clayton.

Aaron looks up for the first time. He glances angrily at Victoria. Every member turns to look at him, anger and annoyance crossing their features. He can't blame them.

"If you don't come up, I'll drag you. Wouldn't want to be pulled around by a girl would you?" With her hands on her hips she smiles at Aaron. She is daring him not to walk up on his own.

"As if you can." Aaron is suddenly next to her, whispering in her ear. She jumps and then turns around and crosses her arms.

"Don't do that!" Victoria snaps at Aaron.

"Now as Clayton was saying, the plan is simple." Aaron pauses to take a deep breath. He never thought he would be leading anyone in his lifetime. "We march to Reformation which is directly north of us. It's about a two month long trek if you walk slowly and use the same path I took. Once we arrive, we stake out a few miles away until it rains.

"Once it begins to rain, we take my lead. We will go opposite of the wind and enter the compound. Half will go with me and Clayton into the compound, the other half will go with Victoria."

"After breaking off into the two groups, Victoria's group will head to the training compound. That's where the majority of the Revelation members are going to be. Victoria will be taking the stronger Soldiers with her. Make sure you are ready to die.

"Once we are inside the compound, I will be leaving Clayton to watch over everyone. I am the only once capable of taking Simon out." Aaron finishes his speech. It is the most he has ever spoken to anyone other than Victoria and Clayton. He isn't sure he ever wants to do it again.

"Anyone who is not ready to die or is not willing to go on this march will be forced to leave the compound tonight." Victoria crosses her arms and looks at the crowd, daring anyone to speak out.

"If no one has any objections, we need begin organizing everyone into their groups." Clayton says. He and Victoria begin to separate the Soldiers while Aaron stays off to the side. He has no one under his command. He is just leading them to their death.

Is Jonathan alright? Is he even alive? Did they break him or is he still strong? What should Aaron prepare to see? He hasn't stopped thinking about Jonathan since the announcement.

"Alright, go to bed." Clayton speaks loudly above the individual conversations. "We will begin preparations and will leave in one week." Clayton dismisses the large group.

No one sees Aaron leave. He walks calmly to his room. Once inside, he locks his door calmly, but the tears are flowing faster than he has even seen. He holds his head and heaves as he attempts to breathe. He can't stand. He falls. He sobs as he crawls towards a wall to lean his head on. Hours pass. He is broken. Jonathan is Aaron's weakness.

Aaron can't allow Simon to hurt Jonathan another

moment longer. He needs to save Jonathan now.

He decides he is going to go back to Revelation alone. He knows a large group will be waiting for him. No one else needs to suffer for what he has done.

Black clothing, jacket, and shoes will provide adequate protection for him, and he has a small backpack with water and meat. There is only one thing left for him to do.

After an hour of failed attempts to find Victoria's room, he finally slides in secretly. She is sleeping soundly, and looks perfectly peaceful. He didn't plan to wake her anyway. He feels the need to tell her goodbye.

Victoria,

Go north, following the road until you reach three rows deep of scorched trees. Enter there and you are right at Revelation. Revelation's symbol is on the third tree in the fourth row. Be safe.

~Aaron Stoppa

He feels no need to wake her up to tell her goodbye. He wouldn't leave. She would remind him of all the danger and he would use his brain to understand and listen. However, his heart wins this battle. He slips out of her room, not sure if he will ever see her again.

Trees blur past Aaron. It is impossible to tell one tree from another. He runs nonstop until the first sight of the moon. The second he notices it in the sky, he allows his legs to collapse. He falls to the ground and breathes heavily, gasping for air.

No thoughts pass through his mind. He closes his eyes and continues to breathe deeply. Quickly, sleep takes over for the night.

For the next two nights he has no thoughts running through his head. He needs to run to Revelation as soon as possible. Any thought will slow him down and make Jonathan continue to suffer.

Rarely does he stop to eat or drink. It takes too long. He waits until nightfall to do so. He always collapses from exhaustion the second he stops running. He doesn't care. He only wants to save Jonathan. Even if it kills him, he will meet Simon's threat. He must arrive at Revelation.

On the fourth day, thoughts of Jonathan being tortured invade Aaron's mind. The same torture Aaron experienced creeps into the darkest corners of his mind. He hears Jonathan's screams. Thoughts of Jonathan's burned and cut flesh race through his mind. Tears streak down his face. He heaves as he runs.

He knows he is close to Revelation. He sees the trees he told Victoria to look for. He should continue, but he needs to rest. He must be strong for confronting Simon. For the last time he lays down. The moon is high in the sky, and he looks at it.

This could be the last time he sees the world. He could be killed or caged immediately. Maybe he will take Jonathan's place. He has no idea what to expect. He isn't scared. He has no fear of Simon anymore. He will kill Simon.

15 Jonathan

Aaron's heart slams into his ribs. For ten minutes he has stood before the gate at Revelation's compound. He can't convince his feet to take another step.

A Gelchork howl comes from the distance, lonely and cold. Aaron has heard this sound hundreds of times. He bows his head for a moment and then runs. He knows this howl. It's the howl of a weak Gelchork accepting it's going to die by the Alpha's hand.

He jumps over the large wall. He wants to turn around. He would rather not be in this situation, but he is ready to face his future. He is ready to face Simon to save Jonathan. This time, he isn't afraid of Simon.

He sprints past the training facility. Too many nightmares exist there. Any bad thought will turn him around quicker than anything.

Revelation

Something is wrong. No sniper tried to shoot at him to stop him. Snipers shoot at anything, even Simon when they don't know he should be coming back. They don't aim to kill but to warn.

He pushes the door, and it opens easily. Something is wrong. He takes a few careful steps inside the compound. It could be rigged to explode. That would mean the basement would be destroyed too. Aaron knows Simon wouldn't be able to handle that.

He walks down the hallway, taking a look into the first room. He can't even remember what it is called. Is it the common area? Maybe it is the lounge. It doesn't matter. Aaron no longer has rooms or people to avoid that may or may not hurt him. He is safe. He is going to take Jonathan back with him, so Jonathan can enjoy safety and freedom.

As he checks the rooms for any sign of movement, he allows his mind to go back to the good times he can remember with Jonathan. He runs through the fields to his brother. The grass tickles the bottom of his feet. The white things coming from the flowers and weeds touch his nose and make him sneeze. He laughs. No one would suspect that this would be the last time Jonathan or anyone would hear Aaron's laugh.

He walks down the hall. He tries to open the door he stands before, but he can't reach the lock. A small child isn't meant to walk around the compound. Simon changed him two months ago. Now Aaron thinks he is invincible and can do anything he wants. A puppet spots him trying to open the door. The puppet throws a large knife at Aaron. It lands in Aaron's side and he falls to the ground in pain.

Aaron walks into his old room and sees it has been completely destroyed and covered in blood. Simon must have gone on a rampage and taken out a few puppets. He should feel bad for them, but he doesn't at the same time. After years of punishment and torture, he is kind of glad they are dead.

He walks into every room in the compound and finds nothing. Blood spatters cover the walls or floors. Puppets are being destroyed left and right because of him.

There is no place to go anymore. There is only one place left to check, the basement. He hates the basement. Screaming and bleeding are his only memories of the basement. If he has the chance, this will be the first place he destroys in the compound.

His heart pounds violently. His pulse can be felt in every part of his body. There is a pounding in his head. He steps in time with his own heartbeat. He places a hand on the door handle and twists it. He pulls the door open slowly. A loud squeak is heard.

He stands there, looking down the stairs. There is no light at the bottom. Only a small glow of light is visible on the far left of the room. He can hear breathing, but there is no movement.

Slowly, he takes the first step on the metal stairs. The people down there will have no doubt he is coming. Aaron is almost positive Simon and Jonathan are down here, but he isn't sure where the puppets are there.

He takes slow, careful steps down the stairs, waiting for

the first step's echo to disappear before taking the next. He wants to turn around and run. He wants to return to the safety of Reformation, but he can't. He must do this. He must save Jonathan.

He takes the last step off of the stairs, and turns to the left. He sees Jonathan on his knees, looking at the floor. He is shirtless and broken. Cuts and slashes cover his entire body. His left shoulder is completely destroyed and burned so badly the bone is completely visible. He has been brutalized and beaten. His bones are showing through his skin. Aaron's heart sinks, but he tries not to show it on his face.

He looks around and sees Simon and around thirty puppets. He wants to walk towards them and start taking them out, but he doesn't.

"Jonathan." Aaron's voice is firm, no longer shaky as it used to be in the past. Jonathan's head slowly rises and his eyes meet Aaron's. A large smile crosses his battered face.

"Aaron." Aaron smiles and takes a step closer to his brother, but then Simon moves suddenly. Simon draws out a knife and slices Jonathan's throat.

Jonathan falls the short distance to the floor, a smile still on his face as he closes his eyes and bleeds out.

16 Aaron

Rage boils through Aaron's veins. Vibrations course over his entire being. Anyone within ten feet of him can feel the anger coming off of Aaron.

"Jonathan!" He picks up his dying brother, cradling Jonathan in his arms. Jonathan is already cold. Death has taken him from the world with a smile still on his face, a smile that will haunt Aaron for the rest of his days.

Aaron sucks in a shaky breath, and gently lays Jonathan's cold body on the floor. He stays kneeling, and whispers a few words to himself before standing. Clayton's beliefs have worn off onto Aaron in the past few weeks.

"Forgive me Lord for the murders I am about to commit, but I don't care anymore." With this prayer, he stands and looks above him. He closes his eyes and allows the rage to take over.

His eyes are what make him special. The lilac purple

with six block dots spaced evenly around the edge of his eye color is different from the normal blue or brown eyes everyone else seems to have. The black dots begin to swirl clockwise, slowly at first, but as he becomes more enraged, they begin to spin faster until there is a twirling black circle at the edge.

He looks down and a small smirk crosses his face. None of the puppets or even Simon himself knows what Aaron is capable of now. They will probably think that he is just the same scared little boy who can't talk. He is a true monster, one hiding his evil and ability to kill behind kindness.

Aaron looks at the closest puppet to him and catches him staring at Aaron. The word excellent crosses his mind. He has found his first victim. He turns his entire body to look at the puppet. He is a small boy, but Aaron knows he lacks innocence. He plunged thirty seven daggers into each of his brothers and sisters for target practice. He deserves to die, even if he didn't have anything to do with Jonathan's torture.

The young puppet shakes, caught in Aaron's stare. He can't move now. His fate has been sealed. Aaron's eyes continue to spin. He quickly decides how he will kill them all. He will imagine the pain instead of describing it. Images have always caused greater pain than words.

Images of lightning dance across Aaron's mind, striking trees and causing fires and explosions. A blood curdling scream exits the puppet's mouth. Aaron's smirk grows a little larger. He shouldn't be enjoying this, but he can't stop himself. He has waited too long for this. The puppet begins to twitch and shake all over, frozen in his place, unable to move or escape the pain.

Aaron imagines a large lightning strike hitting him, as it has done only once, and that ends the puppet's life. It is too much for the body to handle.

Aaron can kill without touching. All Aaron needs is a person's gaze, and then the person's fate is decided. The person will die. If Aaron wants to end it quickly, he can freeze the person in place and then snap the person's neck.

All the puppets in the room freeze. Curses come from under their breaths, cursing him and his ability. None of these puppets has been experimented on. Simon refuses to test new things on his best puppets. None of these puppets has any superhuman ability like Aaron. They are normal and as good as dead, but they will fight.

Two charge at Aaron. Instead of killing them directly, he starts throwing punches and kicks, severely brutalizing everyone in the room. Aaron was never taught to defend himself at Revelation, but Reformation did, and no one here would have known.

He stops throwing punches when they bring out weapons. He needs to save his strength to torture Simon. He catches one's gaze, and then the others. He imagines Gelchorks tearing them apart.

Left, right, every direction, the puppets attack him. He dodges their attacks, and catches the gazes of those he can. The puppets are coming through the basement door. That's why Aaron couldn't find them in the compound earlier.

"Electric shock." Images of electricity run through his brain while the puppets' minds are overloaded with the idea of being shocked to death.

His method of killing is effective. Those he can't kill immediately he can freeze and then deal with any danger in front of him.

He feels cuts and tears all over his skin. Small slivers of blood run down the newly opened wounds, dripping in old scars and burns, not able to escape.

"It's a good thing Jonathan is dead." Rage boils inside of Aaron as he looks around to find the voice's source. With all the commotion it could have come from anywhere. "I hated him."

The voice is right in front of him. A young female with a deep voice and an ugly exterior looks Aaron directly in the eye. He glares at her, but chooses not to catch her in his gaze. He waits to see what else she will say. After he thinks she has said enough, he will cause her severe pain. He will make her regret her words.

"He was weak, only focusing on you. I'm surprised he wasn't killed long ago. He was almost as worthless as you."

"He isn't worthless!" He screams at her and catches her eyes. She releases a shocked breath, but can't talk or move. He has silenced her. "I'll save your torture for later." He lifts her and throws her across the room, making sure to aim for a large cement pillar. He watches her fall into an experimental Gelchork's cage. She may not be alive when he comes back to kill her.

The puppets continue to attack him. He is bleeding profusely now. When he paid attention to her, the puppets took advantage of her distraction and caused as much damage as possible. He doesn't care.

He starts to catch all of their gazes, freezing at least fifty puppets. One frozen puppet to his left squeals like a small animal. Aaron takes the puppet's sword and cuts his head off first. He quickly goes through and slices off as many heads as he can. If he can't cut the puppet's head off, he stabs him in the heart or slits his throat. He doesn't care if the puppets die quickly or slowly. He needs them down and out of the way.

Another round of puppets comes at him, and he does the same thing. The sword is dull by this point, so he grabs another. He doesn't care. He wants them dead. They all had a part in Jonathan's murder.

Jonathan didn't deserve to die. He was an innocent bystander. He always has been. He has just been a pawn in Simon's game from being forced into Revelation to losing his life for Aaron's disobedience. Aaron knows he was worth so much more. They were going to be free. They were supposed to experience life in a new way together. Revelation and all of its puppets took that from Aaron.

He only wants to kill Simon. He never planned to kill as many puppets as he already has. The puppets never were and still aren't his main concern. He just wants Simon gone. If Simon hadn't been hated by everyone, started Revelation, scouted out Aaron as the perfect experiment, created Gelchorks, or even existed, none of this would have happened. All of the blood on Aaron's hands is because of Simon. He is the cause of this.

"No!" The puppets scream as Aaron continues to kill. The only method of destruction he has right now is breaking necks. The swords became too dull too quickly. He continues to freeze rounds of puppets and then run between all of them and snap their necks.

Exhaustion is starting to affect him. It's becoming harder to breathe. He is losing a lot of blood. The attacks keep coming his way. Daggers and arrows are in his body. He has no idea how bad his condition is. This needs to end. He isn't sure how much longer he can keep fighting.

No puppets have come in for a small amount of time. Simon must not have any more hidden waiting to ambush Aaron. Only the best are left. He is running out of energy to fight. He notices a limp in his left leg.

He needs a quick solution, something quick, effective, and easy. What can he do? His back is facing the wall of experiments and chemicals. The best of Simon's puppets charge at Aaron. Aaron sprints to the first chemical he can and throws it at the charging puppets, and then another and another, until all of those at arm's reach are gone.

Many of them are stopped. Flesh is melting off and screams of pain and terror are echoing. It's not enough. It hasn't stopped them all.

There is only one option left. He isn't strong enough to take them out one by one. He has to destroy the roof above them to kill them.

He has nothing left to live for. Jonathan is gone. Now he just wants to kill as many of the puppets as he can. He no longer cares if he dies.

He sees matches to his right and grabs them. He lights one. Before he throws it, he catches their gaze. The remaining seven are frozen in place, unable to move and not ready to accept death.

"The heat comes from all sides, causing you to sweat. It's hot. Smoke smothering your lungs. You can't breathe. The flames touch your feet and burn. The fire begins to consume you." Aaron throws the match towards the puppets.

Everything in his world slows down. He knows what is about to happen. The chemicals will react with each other and the match and an explosion will occur. He is ready to die. He has accepted death. He looks to the far side of the room and sees Simon. He is too far from the stairs to escape before the place blows.

His legs buckle underneath him as the match hits the puddle of various chemicals. His vision goes black. Exhaustion takes over. He can vaguely hear the explosion before he is gone.

17 Simon

Light shines over his being from the cracks and holes in the few walls left. A large tree towers over Aaron's body, over the nonexistent roof. There is no longer a ceiling or any supporting beams. Aaron destroyed them all in the last moments of the battle.

Bodies litter the entire area. Aaron took out nearly the entire compound. Some left, some ran, some stayed to fight. Those who did died by Aaron's hand.

His eyes open slowly. The light nearly burns him to look at. He sees three pebbles in front of his face. His vision is blurry and he isn't sure what he is seeing is real. Is he finally dead? For once, has death actually come?

He looks up and sees six branches above him. They contain beautiful green leaves all over them. If this is where he goes after death, he is fine with it. Maybe he can find Jonathan.

He looks to his right and sees three Simons. His thoughts of peace and happiness and accepting death disappear. His vision is blurred. The pain starts to creep into every single cell in his entire body. His eyes burn and his body aches. He wishes he were dead.

He stretches out his arms and tries to crawl towards Simon. It is almost too painful to bear, but he must kill Simon. It is the only way he will achieve peace in his life. He tries to catch his gaze, but it is too painful for him even to attempt. He wants to kill him so badly. Simon backs away from Aaron.

Parts of Aaron's body are charred from the explosion. How long has he been out? When was the last time he moved? Simon looks in worse condition than Aaron, but he also has charred flesh and open wounds.

"Stop." Aaron takes a deep breath. "Don't move." Aaron's voice is hoarse and almost unrecognizable.

"Now, Aaron, why would I do that?" Simon's tone is unreadable. Is it sarcasm?

"You need to die." It pains Aaron to talk.

"No, I really don't. And neither do you." Simon smiles at Aaron.

"What do you mean, Simon?"

"You are my greatest experiment and weapon, Aaron. If you die, I lose you. I have never been able to recreate you after all these years. We are meant to coexist together. You are special." His voice is sweet and caring. It sickens Aaron. Simon is a cruel animal, incapable of caring about anyone.

"No we aren't!" Aaron shouts, causing severe pain in his throat.

"Listen, if I die, I can't see your progress and learn more about you. You will have nothing to live for. I already took your brother.
What more is left? I am your only reason for existence." Simon is telling a partial truth. Aaron can't stand him. Simon must die.

"I hate you." Aaron spits at Simon angrily.

"I love you." Simon is unaffected by Aaron's words.

"We aren't the same."

"But Aaron, we are. We are both destructors. We only destroy things."

"I may kill, but I am nothing like you!"

"Aaron, I made you."

"You pumped me full of hate. Hate toward you. You made me an animal. Unlike you, I can change." Aaron knows he can change. He changed in Reformation, and he can continue to change.

" No one can change. You are made to be an animal. It's in your nature." Simon takes a step backwards, away from Aaron.

Aaron wants to kill Simon more with every word that comes out of his mouth. He wants to rip his head off. But he can't move.

"Now, remember Aaron, I'll always be watching you, until you come to your senses. I may be ten feet away, or half way around the world. I will always know where you are and who you are with. Goodbye."

Simon walks up the stairs and leaves what used to be the basement. There isn't a door anymore. The stairs lead to the wilderness, fifteen feet higher than where Aaron lays. He tries to crawl over and yell stop. He wants to kill Simon. Blackness starts to invade his vision. He loses sight, until he is out cold again.

When he wakes again, movement has disturbed his slumber. Images of puppets coming to kill him cause him to roll over quickly and grab for a weapon. He grabs one of the bloodied swords and looks around. His world spins a little, but his vision is almost back to normal. All he sees are Soldiers walking around, picking up dead bodies. Every direction he looks there are Soldiers. They are all carrying body bags. How many puppets did he kill?

"Aaron!" Victoria fires question after question at him. "Thank God you are okay! What happened? Why did you leave? Why didn't you wait for us?"

He processes what she says, but chooses not to answer. He doesn't care.

He heads towards the one body yet to be bagged. Even the girl thrown in with the Gelchork is bagged. Somehow the Gelchork managed to survive the explosion and only lost a leg. He doesn't care about that.

He walks over to his brother and looks over at him. He can't understand why Jonathan had to die. A single tear flows from his eye as he kneels down next to Jonathan. A small smile still graces Jonathan's face. Aaron can't hold in his emotions. He begins to cry uncontrollably.

Revelation

Victoria rushes over to find out what is wrong, but she can't talk to him. He continues to cry no matter what is going on around him. Everything that has caused him pain that involved his brother hits him hard emotionally.

Aaron Stoppa, Revelation's greatest weapon, the Warrior Weapon, is finally broken.

18   Victoria

A large wooden coffin sits on the ground under the large Redwood, above the destruction of the compound. Inside, Jonathan still holds his smile he showed Aaron. No one dared to touch Jonathan's body.

Aaron stands next to the coffin, an occasional tear sliding down his face. He is in his own world, ignoring those around him. He no longer wants to exist in this world. Simon was right. Jonathan was the only thing Aaron had to live for.

"Hey." Victoria puts her hand on Aaron's shoulder. She has been trying to console him since he woke, but he hasn't allowed her to.

"Hey." Aaron is solemn. He doesn't want to talk to her right now.

"Look, we're going to catch him, Aaron."

"No, we aren't. I will. It's my responsibility. I have to get revenge."

"I can help. So can Clayton, and the rest of Reformation."

"I should do this alone."

"No, you shouldn't, Aaron."

Aaron looks around and sees the bodies that have been yet to be picked up. So many people died here by his hand. He blames Simon. Had he never threatened Jonathan all of these people would still be alive.

"I don't want anyone else to be harmed. So many already have, like Jonathan and Daryl."

"You know, if they didn't have someone to fight for, they wouldn't have become involved in this mess. Jonathan wanted to protect you, and he tried as hard as he can."

"What about Daryl? If I didn't exist, he would still be alive."

"He wanted to protect me. He never wanted me to go into battle. If you hadn't left early, I would have done the one thing he hoped never would have happened. Aaron, you aren't a bad person."

"I'm not a person. I'm a freak." Aaron turns away from Victoria. He lightly punches the tree before Jonathan's coffin. All the life in Aaron was drained during the battle. His clothes are tattered, his body scarred again.

"Aaron, no you aren't," said Victoria. "You're special and strong and full of special abilities this world has never seen. You saved all of us from dying in a battle with enemies we weren't strong enough to fight. You took the pain for us, for Jonathan. A freak wouldn't do that. A freak would stay away from people and enjoy others' pain." Victoria puts her hand on Aaron's shoulder. "You are a person, a good person with a big heart and a strong will."

Aaron says nothing and neither does Victoria. The two stand there for some time in silence. Aaron thinks about everything that has happened in his life.

"We should head back to Reformation." Clayton walks over to them. Quickly after seeing the pair, he points a finger at them and starts to jump up and down. "Aaron and Victoria sittin' in a tree, k-i-s-s—"

Aaron rips off a branch of the tree and hurls it in Clayton's direction. Without Aaron's super speed, no one can dodge the projectile. It hits Clayton in the chest and sends him five feet back before he lands on his back.

"Good job. I was about to go strangle him."

"Sadly we need him, Victoria."

"Yeah, sadly."

"Hey I heard that! Aaron, that really hurt!"

"Oh well." Victoria and Aaron speak simultaneously, neither caring about Clayton's pain. Aaron never wants to think of Victoria like that. He isn't sure he would want a female counterpart in his life other than a friend like Victoria. This isn't a world he wants a child to live in. Simon would hunt the kid down and kill or experiment on the kid to see if Aaron's experimentation passed through the genes.

Revelation

Aaron looks at Clayton, who is still recovering from the tree branch. Victoria has gone over to help him, but Aaron just shakes his head. He looks at Jonathan's coffin. He can't believe Jonathan is gone for good. He wanted to show him a world where there is no pain or suffering. He wanted to see it with his brother. Simon took that opportunity away from him.

"Simon, I will hunt you down and kill you. Whether it takes me five months or a hundred years, I will make sure you are dead." Aaron whispers to himself while standing over Jonathan's coffin. "I swear on my brother's grave I will kill you for killing Jonathan."

"Aaron we need to go! It's a long walk back and I'm already tired from walking here." Clayton is dusting his pants off, ready to leave.

Aaron lifts his brother's coffin on the ground and slings it perpendicular to his neck. He uses both arms to brace it straight onto his neck. He will be the one to carry his brother to Reformation. It's no one's responsibility but his own.

They all walk away from Revelation's remains. All of the dead puppets are left in body bags. Clayton and Victoria wanted them burned, but Aaron doesn't have the heart to do that. Even the evil ones in the world should have a right to know if their friend or relative is coming back or if they died by Aaron's hand. Word should spread quickly that the main Revelation compound is gone and Simon is missing or at another compound. Everyone in Reformation needs to be on the lookout for new information about Simon's whereabouts.

Victoria, Clayton, and Aaron are at the back, watching all five hundred members of Reformation walk. Not one of their men died today or on the way. Compared to the nearly thousand dead at the compound behind them, Aaron feels like one thing was accomplished. For once, everyone is going home.

Growls come from their right. No one reacts but Aaron. Those growls aren't dinner or any game Reformation is used to. Quickly he sets down the coffin behind him and crouches, ready to attack. Gelchorks that have been set free are now wild, listening to the Alpha.

A large pack of at least sixty Gelchorks comes from the woods. No one in Reformation knows what to do. They have never seen one before. The eight foot tall mutated dogs with heads that split open aren't hard to miss. Intimidation leaks from the holes in their burnt flesh and the holes where spinal bones stick through their back.

They are hungry. Aaron has seen them feast. The mass of Reformation Soldiers will be appetizing to the pack. He can't allow them to take out anyone. If anyone is injured or dies, it should be Aaron. He is the reason they are here. He may not like everyone at Reformation, but he will die to protect everyone.

A growl comes from the Alpha's mouth, so loud it moves branches from the Redwoods ten feet behind Aaron. Aaron isn't intimidated by the Gelchorks. At one time he connected with them. Now, he is going to break them.

He sprints towards the Gelchork, stopping directly in front of its nose within half a second. He then sprints to its tail end in the same amount of time. The Gelchork can't keep up with Aaron's speed. As the Gelchork tries to turn around, Aaron jumps onto its back and lands near the top of its head. He quickly grabs the snout and twists quickly to the left, snapping the dog's neck within seconds.

All the other Gelchorks behind him howl and lay down. Their Alpha is gone and so is their confidence. There is no Beta in this pack. There never has been. The one who takes out the Alpha is the new Alpha. In this case, now Aaron is the new master.

Aaron turns to Victoria and Clayton, and then the rest of Reformation. Murmurs spread throughout the Soldiers.

"Aaron, what is that?" Fear is present amidst the curious tone
in Victoria's voice.

"Gelchorks, another of Simon's experiments." This is no news to Aaron, and he refuses treat it as such.

"There are more than just you?" Clayton is astonished. Aaron nods sadly.

"We need to go back to Reformation. It's time for the hunt to begin."

Aaron lifts his brother's coffin once again, and then, unfazed, walks through the crowd of Soldiers to the front. He is going to lead the way back to Reformation. He knows the woods. He is going to make sure every Soldier makes it back.

As he walks, he never looks back to see if he is being

followed. He can hear everyone behind him. Before, he was scared and alone on this very same journey. This time, he isn't. He isn't surrounded by friends, but he also isn't surrounded by enemies. He will have support now. Everyone here is ready to take out Revelation. With Reformation, Aaron will be able to hunt down Simon. Simon can't hide from an army.

Until Simon is dead, Aaron will only be concerned with hunting him down.

End Book One

Made in the USA
Charleston, SC
24 February 2014